Lock Down Publications and Ca$h
Presents

A THUG'S STREET PRINCESS 2

Written By

MEESHA

First Edition 2024

Printed in the United States of America

This is a work of fiction. Names, characters, places, and incidents either are products of the author's imagination or are used fictitiously. Any similarity to actual events or locales or persons, living or dead, is entirely coincidental.

Lock Down Publications
P.O. Box 944
Stockbridge, GA 30281
www.lockdownpublications.com

Like our page on Facebook: Lock Down Publications
www.facebook.com/lockdownpublications.ldp

Stay Connected with Us!

Text **LOCKDOWN** to 22828 to stay up-to-date with new releases, sneak peaks, contests and more…

Like our page on Facebook:
Lock Down Publications

Join Lock Down Publications/The New Era Reading Group

Visit our website:
www.lockdownpublications.com

Follow us on Instagram:
Lock Down Publications

Email Us: We want to hear from you!

Chapter 1

Breeze

Being in bed after such an adventurous day was so relaxing. Taz was wrapped around my body like I was going to sneak out in the middle of the night or some shit. We arrived at my house from the block party and I gave her lil ass the business after we showered. Taz was sleep soon as I made her see stars from the explosive nut she busted. I stared at her like a creep in the night until my eyes grew heavy and I could no longer keep them open. In no time I was snoozing just the same. My rest was interrupted when my phone rang. I pulled Taz's arm tighter around my waist, running my thumb across it as I tried my best to ignore the sound coming from the device. When it stopped, I thought I would finally be able to sleep, but I was wrong because it sounded once again.

"Breeze, answer that damn thing," Taz said groggily.

"Fuck that phone and whoever is on the other end of it. I'm sleep." Soon as the words left my mouth the ringtone replaced my voice.

"Got dammit, Breeze! Answer the phone before I do," she snapped. "It's damn near five in the morning for God's sake. Sia bet not be the muthafucka blowing your shit up."

"Sia has no reason to dial my phone under any circumstances. Please don't start that jealous shit with me. I'm lying in the arms of the woman I want. You have to trust me, Taz."

I reached toward the nightstand and ran my hand over the surface until I located my phone. The last thing I wanted to do was argue about why I refused to answer my phone. Rolling over on my back, I used face recognition to unlock the device and it immediately rang for the third time. I didn't recognize the number but that didn't stop me from answering.

"Hello," I said clearing my throat.

"Hi, um, I'm sorry to wake you, but I found your number in a phone and I think—"

"Hold up, how does one just so happen to find a number in a phone?" I asked cutting the woman off midsentence. "Baby, I don't play the woman-to-woman games so, I'm telling you now, I have no dealings with Sia. Make this your first and last time contacting me." The line went silent and pissed me all the way off. I opened my mouth to cuss her ass out but her words stilled my tongue instantly.

"I'm sorry, I don't know who you're talking about. This call isn't about anyone named Sia. You need to come to University of Chicago Hospital soon as possible. The emergency room is located on 56th and Maryland."

I jumped out of bed with the phone to my ear and headed straight for the closet. Snatching a pair of joggers from a hanger, I used my shoulder to keep the device in place. My heart was beating erratically as I dressed. It dawned on me that I was bent out of shape and didn't even know who was in the hospital. "Who told you to call me?" I asked throwing a shirt over my head.

"I search the phone and decided to call you because the contact said *Sis*. There was an incident and Cheno was transported to the hospital by ambulance."

Hearing Cheno's name stopped me in my tracks. Tears stung my eyes and I fought to hold them back. I hadn't shed a tear since burying my mama, but my brother being hurt broke me. Taking a deep breath so I wouldn't hyperventilate, I paced.

"He told me to get his phone before he lost consciousness."

"Loss consciousness? Is my brother alright?" I asked nervously.

By this time Taz was out of bed getting dressed as well. The conversation on my end would alert anyone that something was definitely wrong. She too was concerned and I didn't know what to tell her at this point because all I knew was that my brother was rushed to the hospital.

"I don't know. The paramedics told me what hospital they were transporting him to, and I followed in my car. The doctors rushed him to the back soon as they arrived, and I haven't heard anything more."

"What happened?"

I was frantically searching for my keys but my mind went blank. All I could think about was the last conversation I had with Cheno at the block party. I regretted not telling him I loved him before we went our separate ways. A lone tear rolled down my cheek and Taz was there to wipe it away.

"My name is Danica. I will stay until you get here, and I can fill you in on what I know."

The call ended and all types of questions were running through my mind. Where was Cheno when the incident happened? Did he crash his bike? Who was the woman that called? It was chaotic for me mentally and I felt as if I was about to have a breakdown.

"Sit down for a second, Breeze." Taz guided me to the bed. She bent down and eased my foot into one of my slides. Doing the same to the other, Taz rubbed my calf to try calming me. Standing, Taz gathered me in her arms, hugging me tightly. "What hospital is he at?"

"University of Chicago in the city," I whispered.

"Come on. I'll drive." Taz held my hand as we left the bedroom. She made sure to lock up before we made our way to her car. As we got in and buckled up, I couldn't focus on anything she said to me. "Snap out of it, baby. Cheno is going to be alright. Call Charlie and Honey," she said backing out of the driveway.

I started sobbing because I didn't know if my brother was going to be alright or not. I was used to being strong in most situations, but being strong wasn't an option in that moment. Making the call to Honey and Charlie was something I didn't want to do. I knew I didn't have a choice unless I wanted to get cursed out for not doing so. Contemplating if I should wait until I had more information or not, I bit the bullet and called them both on Facetime. Honey joined first then Charlie not too long after her.

"Breeze, it's early as hell," Honey said rubbing her eyes. She must've saw the redness of my eyes because she sat up and turned on the lamp beside her bed.

"What are you crying for?" The two of them asked simultaneously.

"I'm on my way to University of Chicago on Cottage Grove. Something happened to Cheno. I won't have any answers until I talk to the doctors. I need y'all right now."

"I will meet you there. Drive carefully, Breeze," Honey said.

"Give me a minute and I'll see you soon. Stop crying, sis."

I was afraid to speak so I just nodded in response to what they said. There was no point of me being on the call any longer so I just ended it. Taz was tearing the expressway up since we had nothing but opportunity because majority of the city was still sound asleep on a Sunday morning. I was shifting around, wishing I had brought one of my many blunts out of the house with me. If I was in my own vehicle, the weed would've been at my disposal. My anxiety was through the roof without my medicine of choice.

I started rocking, tapping my hand on my knee, and biting my already short fingernails. It was something I did when my nerves were on edge.

Taz picked up on my movements right away. "There's three in the cupholder along with a lighter. I knew you would need it. Let the window down. You get a pass to smoke in here today only." Taz looked at me and smiled.

"You know me so well. Thank you, baby."

The smoke filled my lungs with ease and I held it in as long as possible, closing my eyes. The effects of the cannabis relaxed me instantly. At least for the time being. The moment the hospital came into view, my nerves started going haywire once again. I took long tokes of the blunt trying to get back to the space I was in a few minutes earlier. It wasn't working. Seeing my brother alive and well would be the only thing to ease my mind.

My thought process throughout was to jump out of the car as soon as Taz pulled into the parking lot. Instead, I couldn't move. I was terrified about what awaited inside the building my brother was in. Cheno was all I had left since my mama was no longer with us. He was my best friend, my protector, and the only person I loved with all my heart and soul. There was no way I would be able to function properly without anger if he didn't make it out of this okay. I shook my head to rid my brain of the negativity.

Cheno was somewhere in that hospital. His condition was unknown but I was thinking of life without him. I couldn't fold that easily because he didn't groom me to be weak. Finishing off the blunt, I plucked the roach out the window. I reached within myself and summoned my inner strength to carry me through.

"You ready?"

"Ready as I can be. I can't find out anything sitting out here," I responded.

Opening the door, I stared at the emergency entrance through the windshield. Taz walked around the car and took hold of my hand. As we walked across the parking lot, Honey's voice filled my eardrum.

"Breeze!"

She was backing into a parking space. We waited for Honey to join us and she embraced me in a hug before we made our way to the entrance. The automatic doors separated, inviting us inside. My mouth started watering and I felt sick to my stomach. The night my mama died came back full circle. Everything around me seemed like it was moving in slow motion. The front desk appeared to be miles away, but I approached it faster than my mind expected.

"How can I help you?" the nurse asked.

"My brother, Ricky Woods, was brought in by ambulance sometime this morning. I'm his sister. Is there any word on his condition?"

"Ricky Woods, you say?"

I nodded and the nurse began typing on the keyboard. After a while, she stopped as she read what came up on the computer. "Mr. Woods is still in surgery."

"Surgery? What is he in surgery for?" I asked.

"I'm only permitted to give information to immediate family."

At that point irritation set in because, when I addressed her, the first thing that came out of my mouth was, *"My brother"*. Instead of going off, I pulled my identification from my pocket and handed it to her. She looked over the information longer than needed.

"Ricky is my brother. Please tell me what happened to him," I pled.

She glanced over my ID once more before finally giving me what little information she could. "Mr. Woods was indeed brought in a little after four this morning with several gunshot wounds. He's in surgery and there hasn't been any updates as of yet. You can take a seat in the waiting area and someone will be out to talk with you when new information is available." She typed while glancing at my ID then handed it back to me. "I've added you to his file as his primary contact person. Is that alright with you?"

"That's fine. I'm his emergency contact anyway," I replied scanning the waiting area. When I couldn't figure out what I was looking for, I turned my attention back to the nurse behind the counter. "I have a question. The woman that came in with my brother, is she still here?"

Standing to her feet, the nurse did exactly what I did. She scanned the waiting area. As she studied the individuals that were seated, she pointed in the direction of a woman sitting by the window. "Yes, she's the one sitting alone with the red shirt and jean shorts. I can honestly say that woman is worried sick about your brother. She has been asking about him constantly, but I couldn't give her any updates."

"I'll update her. Thank you for your help," I said walking away with Honey and Taz close behind.

"Breeze, wait. Who was with Cheno?" Honey asked.

"I don't know but I'm about to find out."

I made my way across the room swiftly and the automatic doors caught my attention. Charlie entered frantically and I redirected my steps toward her. She too hugged me as if I was fragile, causing me to pull away.

"What's going on, Breeze?" She asked with a nervous tone.

"Cheno was shot. He's in surgery and that's all I know right now."

I went on to tell her the information I'd obtained from the nurse then filled them in on the phone call I had received from Danica. I made the mistake of pointing in Danica's direction and Charlie zoomed in on her like a hawk surveying its prey. Her thoughts were probably the same as mine about Danica. *Who the fuck is this chick?* Charlie walked away and headed straight for Danica. I knew she was about to go clean off on her ass.

"Hold up, Charlie," I said trying to stop her from causing a scene.

"For what?" she asked spinning around angrily. "I need to know how she's involved in all this. Cheno is lying on an operating table and she is sitting out here without a scratch. The bitch got some explaining to do and I want to hear what she has to say for herself."

Charlie made a point I didn't even think about. I still couldn't allow her to go bat shit crazy on the girl. Honey blocked Charlie's path to prevent her from going further up the aisle toward Danica.

"Listen to me, Charlie. This is not the time nor place to question this woman about anything other than what happened to Cheno."

"That's all I'm going to discuss. What and who Cheno does is no longer my concern." She pushed pass Honey, drawing Danica's attention.

She stood with a forced smile as we got closer. I cut through a row of chairs and still couldn't get to the woman faster than Charlie.

"You must be Cheno's sister. I'm Danica." With an outstretched hand she introduced herself to Charlie.

One would have thought Danica was trying to smear shit on her or something. The look of disgust was on full display for everyone to see and Charlie didn't try to hide it either. "Nah, I'm not, but tell me what went down with Cheno, and don't leave nothing out."

I stepped in immediately to defuse the situation. "Hi, I'm Breeze. Cheno's sister. Thank you for calling to inform me about my brother. I'm sorry for the hostility. We are all worried about Cheno right now."

"I don't need you to apologize for me. I said what the fuck I said. Now, get to talking. How did Cheno end up shot and who did it?" Charlie barked.

Danica didn't appear fearful at all. In fact, she looked ready to jump in the ring with Charlie. The bullshit was gonna have to wait because a scene was something we were not going to cause in the hospital. I thought taking the conversation outside would be a better option for us all. Plus,

I wanted to smoke while hearing what my brother went through.

"I think we should go to the parking lot. Tension is too thick and we can use some fresh air. Do y'all agree?"

"It's alright with me," Danica retorted. "Let's be clear, though. I'm not here to argue or fight anybody. There damn sho won't be nobody screaming in my face either. I stayed here to talk with you. I know the relationship between you and your brother. The way you are coming for me tells me you're the girlfriend." Danica addressed the last statement directly at Charlie.

"Nah, I'm the ex, but none the less he's still my business," she said with lots of venom in her tone.

"Save the attitude for the next bitch. I don't know Cheno outside of trying to save his life, so you can get that bitter taste out ya' mouth." Danica walked away and out of the hospital smooth as hell.

I was impressed because she shut that shit down before it could start. Charlie was not too happy about how she was handled. To be honest, I was glad she had no dealings with Cheno because it would've for sure turned into a boxing match.

"Who did she think she was checking? I will put my foot so far up her ass—"

"Control your emotions, Charlie," Honey snapped at her. "The girl said she don't even know the man like that and you still big mad. Every woman doesn't want to stoop to your level and fight when you in your feelings. Cheno is possibly fighting for his life and the only thing you care about is who he's fucking. You gotta do better. Aren't you the one that told him never to contact you again?"

"I won't go there with you because we're better than that. Our emotions are all over the place and I don't want to say something that will tarnish our friendship. I'm telling you now, if the bitch says the wrong thing, I'm knocking her the fuck out."

"Practice growing the fuck up, first. One of these days you gon' learn fighting isn't always the answer." Honey headed for the automatic doors and I couldn't do nothing but shake my head.

I opened my mouth to voice my opinion to Charlie and Taz stepped in and kissed me. Charlie gave us some privacy and left the hospital as well. The distraction from my girl was just what I needed in that instance. All I wanted to know was what happened to my brother. The other shit they could keep.

When we got outside, Danica was standing at the far end of the walkway talking on her phone while Honey and Charlie exchanged words lowly between them.

The events that led to my brother being shot was my main concern, so I went to speak with Danica. She saw me coming and ended her call too fast for my liking. Her actions were suspicious, and I prayed she had nothing to do with what happened to Cheno because I wasn't a killer, but don't push me. I would slump her ass right outside the hospital if need be.

"You didn't have to end your call on account of me," I said when I got closer.

"No, I had to call and check on my kids. My mama went over to get them ready for school since I'm here."

"How many kids do you have?"

"Girl, five. I love every last one of them, too."

Danica having five kids let me know she in fact wasn't dealing with Cheno on a personally level. There was no way he would fuck with her because she was fertile, and he wasn't trying to play stepdaddy to nobody's offsprings. Cheno didn't believe in taking over the job another nigga created. There was an incident in Georgia when he took a female on a date. When he dropped her off at home, she invited Cheno inside and kids started running from every room in the house. His stupid ass left that house fast and blocked her number before he started his car. I laughed real tears as I listened to him tell the story.

"Breeze, look, I'm sorry for how I acted in there. I just didn't like the way your friend tried to check me. Cheno is a stranger that needed my assistance this morning. That's all."

"You don't have to explain anything to me, Danica. What I want to know is what happened."

"I can't tell you what led up to him getting shot, but I can tell you what happened during and after."

She looked down at the ground and I waited patiently while she gathered herself to continue. Taz and the others joined us. Charlie still had the resting bitch face as she glared at Danica. Shaking my head, I let her know I wasn't with her bullshit. She was not about to interrupt me hearing about my brother getting shot. In response Charlie smacked her lips and waved me off.

"I live on 71st and Michigan. When I was getting ready for work, I heard an accident outside and I ran to the window to see what was going on. There was a car smashed against the light pole with the other car resting against the passenger door. I automatically called 911 as I dressed to go assist any way I could. The operator was asking questions I couldn't answer and I cussed her out and told her to send an ambulance."

"How did a car accident turn into my brother being shot?" I asked confused.

"I was looking to see if there were any movement in the vehicles then the old school Chevy's driver door opened and a man got out with a gun in hand. He shot until the clip was empty and I was frozen in place. When I kept hearing the clicks, I hollered out the window that I called the police. The nigga couldn't see me and said if he knew where I was, he would shoot me, too. He got back in the car he rammed into Cheno's and drove away with his bumper dragging on the ground."

The entire scene played in my mind like a movie. The old school Chevy came back to me and the shit Cheno said about his trap. The muthafucka that stole from him was behind this shit. Murder was on my mind because I had to find out more about this hit on Cheno's life and his trap.

"I ran out the house and to his car as fast as I could. When I got inside his car, there was so much blood. All I could do was try to keep him awake. At that point, I tried to get as much information out of him and all I got was his name and the phone. The ambulance came a few minutes later and he was whisked away. I was questioned by the police and I gave them the story I just told you." Danica dug around in her purse and pulled out Cheno's phone. "Here is his phone. I only went through the contacts. You may want to see if there's any valuable information in there. I don't fuck with the police, so I gave them his keys. Oh, this was in the car too," she said turning her back to hand me Cheno's Glock.

"Good looking. I appreciate you on all levels. Thank you for trying to save my brother's life."

"I would want someone to help a member of my family the same way. I was scared but my fast action was necessary. I just hope it saved his life. Is there anything else I can do for you?"

"Nah—"

"Yeah, I got one," Honey interjected. "I've never heard Cheno say anything about having business on 71st. Are you sure you didn't know anything about him before this morning?"

"I'm more than sure. If there was anything more between us, I would stand on that shit. That man was fine as hell, now that I think about it." Danica chuckled. "No disrespect to you." She nodded in Charlie's direction.

"None taken. You not his type anyway."

"Pussy isn't a type. They all get wet, squeeze a dick tight, and can make a man come back for more. Don't get it twisted, boo. Unfortunately for you, I'm not part of the threat you're so ass-hurt about. Breeze, it was nice meeting you."

Danica walked away and I was so glad to see her go. Charlie was ready to tear her head off for that last statement. I was laughing my ass off because her comebacks were wicked. She didn't lie at all. Sometimes the truth hurt, especially when a stranger hit you with your life story without actually knowing.

"I told you to leave that shit alone. That shit stung a little bit, didn't it?" Honey asked as we made our way back to the waiting area.

"Fuck you, Honey."

"I will when all the hoes in Chicago do the same."

The two of them were about to be at it for the rest of the morning. That was between them because my name Bennett and I ain't in it. I went to the counter to see if there was any news on Cheno and it wasn't. For the time being, all I could do was pray and wait.

***

I was hungry just sitting in wait. Honey, Taz, and Charlie left because business stopped for no one. Taz caught a ride with Honey and left the car with me. The need to go home and freshen up was highly on my mind. It was almost eight in the morning, and I was tired as well. I couldn't leave without finding out the status of my brother. No news was good news most of the time and I kept that in mind. Making my way to the counter, there was a different nurse there.

"Good morning. I'm waiting to hear word on Ricky Woods. I know there isn't an update, but I need to go out to grab something to eat and take a shower. Can you please have the doctor give me a call if I'm not back?"

"Sure, we can do that for you. First, I will need to get some information from you."

"Everything you need to know is in his chart. My name is Breeze."

"Okay. I will make sure you're contacted soon as the doctor has any news."

"Thank you."

My intuition was telling me to stay, but the way my mouth felt told me to leave and freshen up. Hell, I didn't even think I brushed my teeth before leaving the house after the call I'd received. It was hot as hell on that late July morning. I was sweating before I was even halfway across the parking lot. Fishing the keys out of my pocket, I started the car with the fob. As I continued to walk, Cheno's phone started to ring. I pulled it out without checking then answered.

"Hello."

"Hey. Where's Cheno?"

"Who is this?" I asked as I opened the driver door and got in.

"This Quell. Who is this?"

"It's Breeze. I was going to call you. I just couldn't make myself go into Cheno's phone to do so. He was shot this morning, Quell. My brother has been in this hospital since a little after four this morning and I don't know how he's doing."

"Nah, not my nigga. Look, what hospital you at?"

"I just pulled off but he's at the University of Chicago." The line went silent and I wasn't sure if he hung up or not. "Quell, are you there?"

"Yeah. I just pulled up to his crib because he did all the leg work on my spot. We made plans for me to pick the keys up from him."

"Stay there. I'm on my way to you."

"Aight, bet. Do you know what happened?" he asked.

Going over the details Danica told me, Quell listened silently. I voiced all of my concerns and how I believed the shooting was connected to the robbery of the trap. Cheno was skeptical about Bam being involved and the same with Lil' Mike. I didn't call none of them niggas because I didn't trust nobody in his camp. Fredo couldn't even be trusted at this point, even though he hadn't given me the vibe of being vindictive towards my brother.

"What do you know about this nigga Tank?"

"All I know is he is related to Cheese. I've only heard that name through Cheno."

"This shit is getting out of hand. I was supposed to been there to watch that nigga's back."

"You can't blame yourself, Quell. Cheno left his house for a reason. He didn't even do business on 71st. Somebody lured him in that direction. I'll be there in about twenty minutes. I gotta make a call."

"Alright, sis. Drive safely and watch your surroundings."

"Will do," I said hanging up.

There was someone I needed to call but it could wait. I wanted to use the time driving to think over some shit alone. Cheese and his cousin were on the top of my list of suspects. Bam didn't show up at the trap because of a call he supposedly received telling him not to show up. Lil' Mike didn't get beat up or shit, and all the product and money was taken. If that wasn't an inside job, my name wasn't Breeze Woods. It dawned on me that everybody was at the block party except Free. The radar in my head started going crazy. Cheno would only leave the house if it was important.

I pushed the gas pedal and sped on the expressway to hurry to the south suburbs. I made it to my house in record time. Hopping out of Taz's whip, I rushed into my house and grabbed the spare key to Cheno's. He lived five minutes from me so it didn't take long for me to pull up.

Quell was leaning against his truck on the phone. "I need y'all in Chicago soon as possible. I have more than enough room for y'all to stay at my crib. Cheno's business is going to run as if he is still up and moving. Let me know what day y'all will be flying in and I'll be at the airport to scoop y'all. Bet." Quell put his phone in his pocket and pushed off the truck.

I rounded the car and gave him a hug. He was like another brother to me, so I was sure Quell understood my mindset at that time. "We gon' get through this, Breeze. The man upstairs has the last say. Cheno gon' pull through because my nigga ain't never about to leave you out here like that."

"I don't know, Quell. I've never known someone to be in surgery long as Cheno has."

"It's very common. That means the doctors doing all they can for him."

I nodded then walked up the stairs to the front door. "Welcome to the neighborhood, brah. Chicago is a drastic change from Texas. The winters ain't no joke," I said, forcing a laugh.

"I'll be straight. Honey gon' keep me warm. How she doing anyway?"

"She's okay," I said pushing the door open. "She loved the delivery you sent a couple weeks ago. We fucked that pizza up! Thank you."

I walked right to the coffee table drawer and took out the paperwork and keys for Quell's home. The address was on display, and I started laughing hysterically. Cheno wasn't shit but when he wanted something to happen, he went the extra mile to make sure to get the ball rolling.

"What the hell you laughing like that for?" Quell asked.

"You're about to be living right next door to Honey."

"I know. Who do you think picked out the crib? Nah, for real, Cheno sent me pictures and I liked what I saw then decided I wanted the property. He didn't tell me until after the fact that my future wide lived next door." He smirked. "Soon as she stops fighting what's meant to be, we gon' combine them bitches into one house. She just don't know the plan yet. You bet not tell her, either."

"I don't have shit to do with that. Hopefully, she doesn't hurt your heart in the process. Honey isn't ready to mingle. She's been isolated too long. Give her some time."

"Hell, I stayed away for two months! How long do you expect me to wait?"

At that precise time, my phone rang and I started shaking badly. I pulled it out and an unknown number was on the display. I answered and dreaded the call soon as I said hello. Listening to what was being said on the other end, I cried silently. "I'm on my way."

Chapter 2

Jaquellis "Quell" Chambers

"Cheno is out of surgery. He was shot four times and is in a coma. The reason there was no information on his condition is because he flatlined twice. The doctors were finally able to get him stabilized and he is resting comfortably in a room. Everyone will be able to visit him today. After that, it will be two to the room."

"Okay, let's go."

Me and Breeze left Cheno's crib to head over to the hospital. I jumped in my truck and she got in a black Lexus. Following her onto the residential street, we rolled along at the speed limit for a few minutes then Breeze pulled into another driveway. I was confused because I thought we were going to the hospital. Breeze approached the driver side of my truck and I lowered the window.

"I have to run inside and freshen up a bit. I'll be out in fifteen minutes flat."

"Do yo' thang. I'll be right here."

I took the time to reminisce on the good memories me and Cheno made together. We met my freshman year at Morehouse College. Me and a couple of my guys were at a frat party and it was lit. We were in desperate need of some weed and Cheno just so happened to be enjoying the vibe while doing his thang as the distributor. He was a young hustler trying to keep money in his pocket and he was at the right place to get it. I copped what I needed to hold me over for the week then went outside to flame up. As me and the homies enjoyed the product, a commotion inside had us putting out the blunts to see what was going on.

"They beating that nigga's ass but it's taking five of them to do it!" Somebody exclaimed from the doorway.

Pushing my way through the crowd, I saw Cheno holding his own while several niggas threw punches at him. There was still a good distance between us but it didn't stop me from trying to get through all the muthafuckas that were just standing around looking so I could aid and assist. One thing about me, I didn't like jumping ass niggas. That shit was pussy to me but they were on the verge of finding out.

"Move the fuck out the way!" My voice boomed out.

The crowd parted immediately, and I went right in taking care of business. My boys didn't disappoint either because at that point, the battle was even. We were fucking that house up! I was hit in the jaw and it only pissed me off more. I turned, grabbed the nigga by the throat and slammed his ass on his back. I commenced to stomping his ass out.

"That's enough, Q," somebody said grabbing my arm.

I snatched away and kicked his ass one more time.

"Gun!"

Gunshots rang out and I made a dash for the side door leading outside. My whip was down the street and that's where I ran fast as I could. After five minutes, none of my homies returned to the car behind me. There was no way I was leaving them behind. We came together, we leave together. I had no choice but to go back to see what was up. Upon my arrival to the house, there were a few females crying on the front lawn and I knew then and there something was wrong. Rushing inside, there was a small crowd in the space where the fight took place.

Cheno was on his knees holding his shirt on somebody's chest. "Where the fuck is the ambulance?" he yelled out in a panic.

My focus was on the pair of Jordan's and I knew right away it was my homie Derek that Cheno was trying to help.

He wasn't moving. Once again, I struggled to get closer to him, but I was pushed out of the way by the paramedics. Derek was pronounced deceased on the scene, and I was the one who had to deliver the news to his family. I lived with the regret of convincing him to go out with me 'til this day.

Cheno and I had a conversation after being questioned by the police. Just know the niggas are no longer breathing to tell how my boy Derek lost his life that day. A friendship was formed, and Cheno been my brother ever since. He believed in my dream of being a tattoo artist and even bought my very first tattoo machine and all the inventory to get started. Cheno also brought clients my way and I became his personal artist. I was part of his organization and kept shit moving in Georgia until I passed the torch a few years ago to move back to Texas.

"You good, bro?" Breeze asked, interrupting my thoughts.

"Yeah. I was just thinking 'bout some shit. You ready to roll?"

She nodded before jumping in the driver seat of her whip.

I remember when Breeze was younger, she always wanted to hang around us. Cheno used to tell her to go play with a doll or something, but Breeze wasn't going. Her little ass made a lot of bread off us playing *Call of Duty* and any other game on the gaming system. Never in my wildest dreams did I think she would grow up to pull more females than the average nigga.

It took no time getting to the hospital. I parked a few spaces down from Breeze and met her in the middle of the lot. She was walking hesitantly, and it caused me to wrap an arm around her shoulder; telling her I had her without verbally expressing it. Breeze laid her head on my shoulder as I guided her to the entrance.

"I'm here to see Ricky Woods," Breeze said once we approached the counter.

The nurse looked up from the paperwork she was working on with a smile. She typed on the keyboard then said, "You can have a seat in the waiting area. Mr. Woods already has two guests at the moment."

"No. I will not take a seat anywhere. Dr. Patel informed me when he called that the entire family would be able to visit today only. I know all about the two visitors at a time rule. That doesn't apply in this case. Now, please, print out the passes so I can see my brother. To be clear, that's me being nice."

"There aren't any notations in his file stating that. I'm sorry, I can't allow you all to go up."

"Bitch—"

I had to pull Breeze away swiftly. I'd seen her in action, and it wasn't anything nice. She was calm until pushed to the limit. It was up to me to de-escalate the situation before it got out of control.

"Ma'am, would you please page Dr. Patel to come down or call for confirmation?" I asked.

Doing as I asked, the nurse picked up the phone. She whispered into the phone mentioning Cheno's name. Nodding at whatever was being said, she ended the call with a sour expression on her face. Tapping on the keyboard, the printer sounded, producing the passes. Without looking at either one of us, she placed them on the counter. "Mr. Woods is in room 728. Take the elevator behind this desk. Have a nice day."

The way the nurse dismissed us was rude, but I ignored her ignorance. As bad as I wanted to address it, I realized it wasn't even worth the argument. Taking the passes, I turned to give one to Breeze and laughed. The mug on her face told a story of its own and she was ready to reach out and touch the bitch.

"Come on, man, before she calls security. Let her make it this time. Bro is waiting on us."

It didn't take long to find the room Cheno was assigned to. Upon entering, my breath got caught in my chest soon as I saw my nigga lying in the hospital bed. Cheno appeared to be sleeping with a tube down his throat. The heart monitor beeped, indicating he was still amongst the living. The cast on his arm caught my attention as well. Cheno was fucked up pretty badly. All the IVs and shit kind of creeped me out but I had to hold myself together so I could be there for Breeze.

I stayed close to her as she slowly walked toward the bed with tears falling from her eyes. The hurt was on full display, and she didn't try to suppress how she felt. Cheno was everything to his sister, so I understood her position.

Honey crossed the room and hugged Breeze. Her red, puffy eyes indicated she too had been crying. I didn't even see who was in the room until that moment. Honey's beauty still stood out regardless of the sadness she was enduring. The man in me wanted to hug her in the same manner she held Breeze but I decided to allow them to have their moment. I turned my attention across the room and noticed Charlie sitting with her hands clasped together in prayer.

"You good, ma?" I asked, taking a seat next to her.

"No. I need him to wake up. I don't want the conversation we had to be our last interaction." She sniffled. "Cheno was wrong and I meant everything I said to him. It just can't end like this, Quell. I wouldn't be able to go a day without thinking about why I left him standing in the middle of the street without hearing him out."

"And it won't be the last conversation, Charlie. Don't count bro out. His vitals are strong and he's still with us. Cheno loves you. He just has a fucked-up way of showing it. Stepping out on you wasn't a good move on his part but his actions didn't stop him from treating you as his number one. You wifey, Charlie."

"Please stop trying to justify what he did, Quell. Right is right, and wrong is wrong. Cheno loving me has never been something I needed to question. Being enough that he doesn't see any other hoe except me is the problem. I've been nothing but loyal to him for years and he always felt the need to have some bitch to fall back on."

Charlie had a point, and I honestly didn't have a comeback to defend Cheno further. I should've kept my mouth closed because I didn't help him at all. Baby girl was hurting seeing him laid up, but she was also hurting for his infidelities. That shit was gonna have to wait because the main concern should've been about Cheno's condition and if he was going to walk out of the hospital on his own two feet.

"Have the doctors been in since you and Honey's been here?" I asked changing the subject.

"Yeah, Dr. Patel came in and explained why he was in surgery so long. Cheno coded twice and they brought him back. He was shot four times. In the right arm, right thigh, and twice in his side. The doctor said Cheno had blood built up in his chest and his lung collapsed. That's why he has that chest tube inserted. It's to drain the blood and any other fluids out of his chest. It's also helping to inflate his lung. They intubated him so he can heal properly, but he has slipped into a coma."

I thought my nigga was breathing on his own but that wasn't the case. They had a muthafuckin' machine assisting in that shit. Long as he was still breathing, that's all that mattered. Hearing what the doctor said eased my mind a little bit because Cheno still had brain activity and his organs were functioning normally.

"Damn. Did he say how long Cheno could be in a coma?"

"According to Dr. Patel, it depends on Cheno. He has to keep fighting. It was pretty touch and go for a while. He said Cheno was very lucky because if the shooter had more bullets, we would be identifying his body in the morgue. He's not out of the woods yet. We have a long road ahead of us."

I was ready to be there for my nigga for the long haul. Seeing Charlie riding as well was something the females of today wasn't built for. Even though Cheno did what he did, his girl was still there holding him down, praying for him to get better. That's what love looked like and there wasn't many out there who would do the same. I watched Breeze sit in a chair beside the bed. She grabbed Cheno's hand and wept. I wished there was more I could do for her, but we had to see this shit through and hope for the best. Whoever did this shit was going to pay in blood and I was ready to make sure of that shit.

"Breeze, you have to stop crying. He can hear you; he just can't wake up right now. Talk to him just like you usually would. Let him know how you feel because he's listening."

Honey hugged her cousin from behind and wiped her tears. Telling Breeze not to cry was easier said than done. I took that opportunity to get out of the room for a bit. I had my own emotions to check. When I rose to leave, Honey watched my every move. As I approached her, I opened my arms and she walked right into them. Honey's body against mine felt so right as if that's where she belonged. The fragrance of her perfume invaded my nostrils, causing me to breathe in deeply.

"Stay strong. Things may seem grim now, but Cheno is a fighter. Being in a coma gives his body a chance to rest, which he needs more than ever. Keep Breeze calm. I'm going to make a few calls and will be back shortly." I kissed the top of her head then stepped back. It was hard for me to take my eyes off her beautiful face, but I managed to pull it together. As I moved toward the door, Honey's angelic voice put a smile on my face.

"Thank you. For everything."

"You're welcome, beautiful."

All the way to the elevator I imagined my lips upon Honey's. When the doors opened I remembered the reason I was in the hospital. Fredo was the only nigga I trusted in

Cheno's circle. It was rightfully my duty to get him up to speed on what was going on. Charlie, Breeze, and Honey had every reason to cry. Cheno was their strength, and he was loved by them and many others outside of his family. It hurt like hell to know my brother died on that table; not once but twice; and the doctors were able to revive him. Cheno's job wasn't done. While he's healing, I was about to shake up his city.

Chapter 3

Cheno

A bright light shined in my eyes, and I couldn't figure out where the fuck I was. The last memory I had was of me driving eastbound on 71st Street to meet that bitch Larisa. Allowing her to send Charlie back to prison didn't sit well with me. Rage was what I felt the closer I got to the police station. My mind zoomed in on how I was going to persuade her to ride with me to my spot for a nightcap. I never made it that far.

Some idiot t-boned me in the intersection, pinning me in my whip. Then I heard gunshots. The hot lead burned through my flesh, and I couldn't do shit about it. Praying was the way to go because a nigga was fighting to breathe. Not to mention, the muthafucka on the other end of the gun wanted my ass dead.

Blood filled my mouth and the metallic taste sure wasn't pleasant. I heard the pussy when he ran out of bullets and peeled away from the scene. Still, I had no control over the situation. A female tried to help, and I gave her all the information I could before I blacked out. That's when I realized I was in a place unknown to me.

The air was crisp and refreshing as I breathed in and out, taking as much as I could get in. The scent of nature at that moment was a smell I'd never experienced before. I felt more alive than I ever had in my entire adult life. To be honest, something wasn't right. It was too quiet and extremely peaceful. I could see the green grass and colorful flowers when I looked downward, but glancing ahead, my vision was blocked by the light.

"Where the fuck I am?"

A nigga was confused because it seemed like I was walking in a circle. The whole time I was going straight as an arrow. Frustration set in, causing me to scream out, hoping someone would approach me for disturbing the peace. Instead, my body convulsed as if I was hit with a high voltage of electricity. Falling to the ground I was shaking uncontrollably. The episode stopped a short while after it started. My heart was beating but it was kind of irregular. The shit had a nigga spooked because I'd never experienced anything like it before.

"Ricky Devonte' Woods."

I stopped in my tracks because there was no way in hell the person who said my name was able to do so. I turned my head slowly to the left and started crying immediately. My mother glided toward me like the good witch from the Wizard of Oz. Seeing her with long, pretty hair flowing behind her reminded me of the days before she was diagnosed with cancer. My mother was beautiful, and the glow that surrounded her frame allowed me to see her fully. Elaine Woods looked healthier than she was the last time I laid eyes on her.

"Ma?" I choked out in an unsure tone.

"It's me, baby. If you wanted to talk to me, all you had to do was start talking. I may not have responded, but I would've heard every word. I see and hear everything you do and say. Getting shot wasn't the way to go." She joked.

"Where are we?"

I was still in shock. As bad as I wanted to wrap my mama in my arms, I was afraid physical touch would cause her to vanish right before my eyes. That was a chance I wasn't willing to take. So, I opted to just keep her talking just to take in her voice long as I could.

"We are in what is called between life and death. I was granted permission to visit with you briefly. We don't have much time though."

I jerked my head back because she sounded crazy, talking about I was in between heaven and earth. My mama basically told me I was dead.

"Ricky, you know better than to look at me like that. I'm not too gone to slap the hell out of you. With all you've done, you're lucky you're not dodging fireballs with the devil instead of being here with me," she snapped. "I told you about the lifestyle you chose to live but you didn't listen. A hard head makes a soft ass and you're feeling the aftereffects. I love you and always will. You need to fight to live. Breeze needs you."

"What do you mean fight for my life? I'm alive!"

"Raise your voice again." She snarled. "Your ass is in the hospital as we speak, lying on a table in the operating room. I saw you doing the Harlem Shake on the ground before I made my presence known. That was the doctor shocking your heart so it would start beating again. A blessing is what I call it. When you make it out of this, do right. I don't want to see you end up on this side; it's not your time. There's a lot more you have to accomplish before you leave the life of the living. I love you, son."

"I love you too, ma. I miss—"

Everything went black before I could get the full sentence out, and just like that, my mama was gone again. It felt like I was falling down an endless hole. It seemed as if I was floating, and the feeling was peaceful. My heart started beating like a drum and I think anxiety was taking over because I couldn't see what was going on around me. I panicked. In my mind I reached out to brace myself but there was nothing within reach to grab. My heart was no longer beating, and for the first time, I was scared shitless. A bolt of lightning flashed before my eyes, causing my chest to burn. In midair my body jerked uncontrollably.

"We're losing him! Increase the voltage." A voice yelled out some distance away. "Clear!"

My body shook for a moment longer. I could feel the patter of my heart and sighed with relief. At that point I landed on the concrete with a thud. I wasn't in an ounce of pain and that was weird because I hit the ground hard and should've been severely hurt from the impact. The scene before me came into view as I blinked rapidly to focus. My senses heightened and I could smell the pungent stench of the westside of Chicago. One could figure out where they were without looking on that side of town.

I stood to my feet and brushed the dirt from my pants. The building to the left of me was one I was unfamiliar with. Niggas were congregating outside of it without a care, and it would've been a good day for them to get caught lacking. Not one of them muthafuckas turned when I walked up, giving me an earful of what they were discussing.

"I fucked Tank's Chevy up and the nigga wasn't even mad."

Everybody laughed, giving the nigga props while he bragged about totaling a whip. What he said next perked my ears like a German Shepard standing guard.

"I rammed that muthafucka into that niggas' shit and hopped out on his ass. Cheno was pinned inside, trapped like a mouse on a glue board struggling to get loose. It felt good filling his body with some hot shit."

As I zoomed in on his face to take in his features, I made sure the shit was etched in my mind because he was going to see me. He was bragging with his chest, but what he didn't know, he was going to beg for his life in due time. They were taking that shit in like they were in the audience of a comedy show. The joke was on them though. *Laugh now, cry later* was the thoughts running through my mind. I turned to see where the fuck I was, and the street signs read 16th and Homan.

"What's the status on the nigga? Is he dead or what?"

"I haven't heard no reports as of yet. The news only reported the shooting, but no other details were mentioned. The way I lit Cheno up, there's no way he survived. I'm confident he's in heaven, playing a harp in angel wings."

"You wild, nigga. How the fuck you catch him, Lord? Cheno ain't never been caught slippin'."

"You asking too many questions. To make a long story short, pussy would lead any nigga out in the open in the wee hours of the morning to get a taste. He fell for the oldest trick in the book and lost his life behind it."

I chortled because I wasn't lured out with pussy. The bitch threatened the love of my life and *that's* what got me out of my bed. The nigga was tweaking like a muthafucka and it was funny. It didn't take the fact away that Larisa conspired on my ass with weak niggas and she was going to die for the part she played. Payback was a muthafucka. All the answers were in my phone and I hoped like hell it was returned to my sister. It was the only time I would be cool with Breeze going crazy in the street. When mad, she was a whole nigga. She would literally turn into the female version of me.

Standing there listening was something I was tired of, so I swung, trying to knock his head off his neck. I missed by a mile. In fact, my fist went through his head, and I stood in confusion at what had just happened. My mama's words rang in my ears. *You are stuck between life and death.* The scene from the movie *Ghost* flashed in my mind when Patrick Swayze was killed. I knew damn well this nigga didn't take me out like that. The conversation continued and I couldn't do shit but take everything in.

"We got a meeting at eight o'clock tonight. Tank and Cheese wants to holla at us about a few things. One I know for sure is if we took care of that nigga Free."

"Oh, that was my assignment and it's definitely taken care of. I took his body to the northside and hung that bitch in an apartment closet on Howard Street. Made that shit look like a suicide since Cheno was already blaming him for setting up his spot. Now both of them niggas turning up with the homies on the other side."

Hearing Free was dead did something to me because I indeed thought he had something to do with my trap getting hit. My nigga was innocent, and I thought the reason he was MIA was because he was dodging my ass. But they had killed him. I'd heard enough and wanted to get away from the westside. When I turned, the sound of a car door closing caught my attention. A big muthafucka with an angry scowl moved toward the group of men. I didn't know who he was, but he looked like someone of importance.

I glanced back at his Range Rover and the license plate read "Tank 16". I mentally took a screenshot of that shit and zoomed in on his features as well because I needed to remember what the fuck he looked like. My list of bodies was getting longer by the minute. No longer wanting to leave, I followed Tank's bitch ass back to his hoes. I had to give it to him, he wore my muthafuckin' money well. These niggas were all over Tank like he was a celebrity. The way Cheese talked about his cousin he wasn't shit in the streets. I beg to differ. This nigga moved like he had some type of rank.

"Quiet down," Tank said above the chatter, glancing around. "As y'all should know by now from Short, there's a meeting at eight. Be there on time. No excuses."

"Where?"

"Where else, Lord?" Tank snapped. "At the warehouse on 27th and Kedzie, nigga! I'm gon' need you to tighten up because you work for me now. All that slackin' shit you were doing on Cheese time is no more. Ain't no three strikes and you out with me. The first fuck up will be your last. Believe that. This goes for everybody, so have ya' shit in order. There's a new Sheriff in town." Tank laughed all the way back to his truck and I was right behind him.

Soon as he opened the door, I jumped in and sat in the passenger seat. Tank drove around for what seemed like hours and I soaked up every location like a sponge to water. The last destination was a single level home in Oak Park. When Tank went inside, I sat where I was and said a silent prayer.

Lord, I know you saved me twice already and I appreciate what you did. The things I have done in my life haven't been the greatest, but you knew what it was when you planned my life before I was created. You see this shit… I mean the things going on down here. A nigga needs to get his lick back. Put me back in, coach, and I swear, whatever you do to me after that, I will have to eat. I won't make any promises…

I guess the man upstairs got tired of hearing me talk because, once again, I was silenced.

Chapter 4

Honey

Seeing Cheno lying in that bed did something to me. Never in a million years did I imagine getting out of jail to spend two months with Cheno. I left the hospital in tears, and hours later, I was still crying. Everything in my home was a reminder of how much Cheno looked after me while I was on lock, and when I returned home. Cheno set me up to survive without him. I didn't know if I would be capable of continuing if he wasn't around. Being strong for Breeze lasted all of fifteen minutes before the roles were reversed. Her tears dried up faster than fluid on a hot Vegas sidewalk when I broke down. She and Charlie insisted I went home to rest, and I took them up on it, too.

I rolled out of the bed and into the adjourning bathroom to get a Tylenol for the massive headache that just wouldn't go away without help. After thumping two pills in my hand, I walked slowly out of my bedroom to go get a bottled water from the kitchen. The pictures I put on the walls leading down the stairs had me emotional once again. Cheno was everywhere I turned, along with Breeze and Charlie.

"Okay, Honey. Get it together. Cheno is going to be alright."

Reassuring myself of that wasn't working. Cheno was in bad shape, and I didn't see any good coming from the situation. In my mind I was planning his funeral on top of wondering who shot him and why. I entered the kitchen and realized the sun had set. The day flew by as I slept. Eating was the furthest thing from my mind, but I needed to get something in my stomach. I grabbed the bottle of water and made my way back upstairs to order some food to be delivered. Door Dash was going to cost me three times the amount I would pay if I went to get the food myself, but I wasn't in the right frame of mind to drive.

My phone was under the sheets, and it took a minute for me to find it. Searching for the app, I placed an order at Nick's because I had a taste for an Italian beef dipped well with hot peppers and mozzarella cheese. There was no way I could eat the sandwich without fries with mild sauce and a strawberry lemonade. The estimated time of delivery was twenty minutes, and I almost cancelled that shit. The damn restaurant was only seven minutes away.

I placed the pills on the dresser so I could take them after I at least ate a little bit. Turning on the TV with the remote, I scanned through the apps of my Apple TV and settled on watching a funny movie on Max. *Little Man* was something I hadn't seen in a long time and the Wayan's brothers knew how to make everybody laugh. Soon as the movie started, my phone rang, prompting me to pause my show.

"What's up, Breeze?" I asked soon as I answered.

"I was calling to see how you doing. Why do you sound like you're still crying?"

"I'm not." I lied. A tear rolled down my face the moment I saw her name on the screen. I wasn't going to admit that shit to her though. "I was just about to watch Little Man while I wait on my food from Nick's. You still at the hospital?"

"Yeah. There's no change. But I've been in here bumping Pac, hoping he would start rapping out of the blue. No such luck yet though." Breeze chuckled. "But when he do, it's gon' be a muthafuckin' party in this bitch, and that's when the fight gon' start because these doctors gon' be trying to put my ass out."

"Breeze, behave yourself up there." I laughed. "Your ass is crazy."

"You ain't seen crazy yet. Just wait until Fredo find out what the streets are saying about the shooting. He came up here after you left. Quell called and told him about Cheno. He thinks Free has something to do with the robbery and knew about the hit. He is nowhere to be found, and mind you, he's been missing for quite some time."

"So, do you know this Free cat?"

"Mmmhmm. I know he used to be loyal to my brother. Free has never come off as a snake to me. Cheno went the extra mile to make sure everybody on his team ate alongside him. What his team did with their money had nothing to do with my brother. If they didn't invest or stack their paper, that was on them. But one of them niggas obviously had their panties in a bunch and couldn't hide the jealousy any longer."

I sat back thinking, and the woman who helped Cheno came to mind. "Aye, didn't ol' girl that called you give you Cheno's phone?" I asked sitting up.

"Yeah, I have it right here, but the muthafucka locked. Cheno's ass was forever changing his code and it automatically locks when the backlight goes off."

"She called you, right?"

"Yup."

"So, how the fuck did she get in his phone to get your number? Breeze, call that bitch, because she's the key to getting in that phone. If she doesn't come up with the information, that means she had something to do with Cheno getting shot."

"Cousin, you might be on point with this one. Hold on, I'm about to call her ass."

I checked for my food as I waited for Breeze to make the call. The driver was at the restaurant, and it was a good thing because my stomach decided to growl loudly. Breeze added me to the call once she had the woman on the phone.

"Hello?"

"Hey, this is Breeze. I met you—"

"Thought you were talking to me, huh? Sorry, I'm not available right now, but leave a message and I'll get back with you."

"This is Breeze, Cheno's sister. Call me when your wannabe funny ass get this message."

Breeze was mad as hell and I couldn't stop myself from laughing. She dropped the woman from the call and called her everything but the Child of God. I needed that laugh because it brightened my day something terrible.

"Who the fuck does that stupid ass shit? I really thought I was talkin' to her childish ass. Now is not the time to be on my bad side. Danity Kane better stop playing with me, and it bet not take her all got damn night to call me back either. Stop all that damn laughing, Honey!"

"I can't. That shit was funny."

"What the fuck ever. I'll call you back when she gets back with me. I need to go outside and smoke before I blow something up."

"Make sure you call me, too. I want to know what's in that phone."

"I got you, even though I know you going to sleep after eating. With yo' fat ass."

"Fat? Yeah, you need to smoke because you and I both know I'm far from fat. Grouchy tail self. Get off my phone, Breeze. Go tend to your addiction."

Hanging up before she could say anything further, my doorbell sounded then my ring notification chimed on my phone. I went to the app to see who was at my door. My stomach did a happy dance as I reviewed the camera. To my surprise it wasn't the Door Dash driver on the other side of the door with my meal. Instead, Jaquellis stood looking good enough to eat with his hands in the pockets of the gray shorts he wore. The tattoo that I fell in love with the first time I saw it peeked out of the side of his wife beater. He reached out and rang the bell a second time, licking his lips as he waited for me to acknowledge the fact he was there. That one motion was sexy as fuck. I was stuck admiring him from the other side of the camera. Giving up on me answering the door, he turned to walk away. To be honest, I didn't want him to leave.

"I'm on my way down," I blurted out to his back.

"You were watching me the whole time, huh?"

I raced downstairs and snatched the door open. Jaquellis scanned my body from head to toe with lust filled eyes. My kitty tingled a little bit as I stepped aside, allowing him entry.

"Do you always answer the door in yo' draws?"

Confused by his question I looked down and wished the floor would open up and take me under. I was standing in front of a man that I swore I didn't want with a pair of boy shorts that barely covered my thick cheeks. The cami didn't help because it couldn't even hide my four pack abs, let alone my ass. I could feel my face heating up as embarrassment set in. I forgot all about coming home, stripping down, and getting right in the bed.

"Oh shit! I apologize. I didn't realize I didn't have on any clothes. Excuse me while I head upstairs to get dressed."

"Don't mind me. This yo' crib. Be comfortable, baby." He smiled, displaying the perfect dimple in his left cheek. "I just came through to make sure you were good."

"I am, but hold that thought. I'll be right back." As I ran up the stairs two at a time, the doorbell sounded. "Would you get that for me?"

"Yup. Go handle yo' business."

Entering my bedroom, I grabbed a pair of lounge pants from the drawer and slipped my legs into them. Shaking my head as I chuckled lowly, I still couldn't believe I'd allowed that man to see me half naked. I looked in the mirror and smiled. My body was still in tiptop shape from when I was in prison. I squared my shoulders and left the room because there was nothing for me to be ashamed of. Hell, I gave Jaquellis a peek under my clothes and he liked it.

I found Jaquellis sitting on the stool at the island, eating my damn fries. He was smashing my shit, too. Usually, I would be upset, but the way he savored the taste of the mild sauce did something to my private parts.

"You just helped yourself to my food, I see." I said sarcastically.

"Man, I called myself stealing one fry and couldn't stop at one. This sauce is the shit! What kind is it?"

"Mild sauce. That's it, that's all." I laughed.

"They don't have this where I'm from. It's good as hell."

"Yeah, I know. Now, give me my food."

I pulled the Styrofoam container away from him and took a seat on the other stool. Tearing the lid off, I stood up, walked into the kitchen and retrieved a knife from the block. The Italian beef was huge, and I knew I wouldn't eat it all by myself, so I decided to share. Cutting it in half and adding some of the fries, I pushed it over to him.

"Thank you for sharing. Any other female would've sat eating in a nigga's face."

"I'm not other females. They don't make 'em like me anymore." I laughed. "I don't mind sharing unless it's a man. I would never share a man." I took a bite of the beef sandwich and wiped my hand with a napkin. "What are you doing out this way? Aren't you staying at a hotel downtown?"

"Nah, Cheno found me a crib and I'm in the process of moving in. That's what I was doing since I left the hospital. You don't remember me telling you I was moving here?"

"I can recall, but I didn't think you would be moving so soon." I said taking a sip of my lemonade.

"Honey, it's been almost two months. It was hard leaving Texas but I'm glad I did. Cheno needs me more than I knew." Jaquellis stared ahead in deep thought after he said Cheno needed him. I could see the hurt in his eyes as I watched him zone out. What happened to my cousin was affecting a lot of people who truly loved him, and Jaquellis was one of those people. His jaw flexed tightly and he balled his fist. The veins in his arm protruded which caused me to reach out to clasp his fist in my small hand.

"We're going to find out who did this, okay?" I whispered.

"I sure am. Fredo is doing a little bit of leg work as we speak." Jaquellis paused for a second then cleared his throat. "Is there something that happened recently with Cheno?"

"Not that I know of. The only incident I can recall is the robbery of his trap…" My words trailed off as I thought back on the night at the club when Cheno approached Cheese about his cousin Tank. I didn't want to believe Cheese had anything to do with the shooting, but I couldn't ignore the possibility of his involvement. Tank was behind the trap incident and Cheno threatened to make him pay. "Cheese. Y'all need to check out Cheese. That would be the starting point to all of this. I'm sure of it."

"Ain't that the nigga from the club? Yo' ex?"

I'd lost my appetite, so I pushed my food away as I nodded. Jaquellis looked at me with pure intensity. I didn't know why I felt guilty because I had nothing to do with Cheese on any level. He was going to see me, though, and he better pray he wasn't behind Cheno getting shot. "Yeah, that's him. Don't worry about going to him because I'll pay him a visit myself."

"You still talking to that muthafucka after how he handled you?"

"No. I haven't seen nor heard from Cheese since that day. But I need to find out if he had something to do with this."

"No, you don't. Me and Fredo gon' get to the bottom of this shit. There's too many snake muthafuckas involved, Honey. The last thing we need is a nigga going after you because of the information you might find. Leave this shit to us."

The headache I had when I woke up was making the back of my eyes hurt. It was so painful I was seeing little white dots every time I blinked. Rubbing my temples with my fingertips, I knew I had to eat the food sitting in front of me.

"You good?" Jaquellis asked.

"My head is pounding. I need to take a Tylenol."

"Not on an empty stomach. Gone head and eat," he said rising from the stool. "Where is your medicine?"

"It's upstairs, but I'll get it once you leave."

"Who said I was going anywhere? You look like you're about to pass out. I'm not leaving until I know you cool. As a matter of fact, gone upstairs and I'll warm your food then bring it up to you."

"Jaquellis—"

"Quell. Call me Quell."

"I'm cool with Jaquellis. Anyway, I don't want you catering to me. I've taken care of myself too many years alone. I'm quite capable of handling it now."

"Well, today you don't have to. Go lay down and I got you."

I was hesitant to allow Jaquellis to roam around my home, but I did what he requested. The way my head was pounding, I didn't have any fight left in me. Grabbing my phone, I left hm to heat up my food and went upstairs. Soon as I entered my bedroom, I climbed into the king-sized bed and snuggled under the covers and closed my eyes. My heartbeat could be heard in my ears, and it only made my head hurt more. I heard Jaquellis when he entered but I didn't budge.

"Come on, Honey. You gotta eat."

Opening my right eye, he stood with my food on a tray that I had no idea I owned, along with a bottled water. Jaquellis placed the tray on the nightstand and helped me sit up. He propped a couple pillows behind my back before putting the tray in my lap.

"Thank you," I said, popping a French fry into my mouth, immediately spitting it out into my hand.

"What's wrong?"

"Reheated fries are horrible. And I thought prison food was worse." I took a long drink from the water bottle. My mouth was watering for those fries and I couldn't even enjoy them. The Italian beef was another story though. I fucked it up in no time flat. Jaquellis watched as I ate with a smile. "Why are you watching me like that?"

"Most females try to eat pretty and shit in the presence of a nigga. You ain't shy at all."

"I've been on a schedule for years and had a time limit to eat. Being pretty while eating won't be something I'm willing to practice. If I look like a pig, so be it." I shrugged while talking with my mouth full.

"Do yo' thang. No judgement here." He laughed. "Where's your remote?" Jaquellis toed off his shoes and climbed into my bed.

I stopped eating and stared daggers into the side of his head. The nigga was comfortable as hell once he found what he wanted next to me on top of the blanket. He was flipping through the Starz app as if he paid the subscription on that bitch. While I was irritated, my pussy had other things on her mind. Settling on *John Wick 4,* Jaquellis adjusted himself against the headboard.

"Comfortable much?"

"Yup. Finish your food because I'm not leaving, Honey."

"I'm finished. Now, you can see yourself out. I don't need a babysitter," I said, picking up the Tylenol then chased it down with water.

Jaquellis paused the movie, got up, and walked around to my side of the bed. I was glad he saw things my way and took heed to what I'd said. He took the tray and left the room. I got under the cover, closing my eyes. My tolerance for medicine was low so the pill started to kick right in, making me sleepy instantly. When I felt the bed dip and the movie started again, I didn't have the energy to argue about him being back in my bed and not on his way to his own damn house.

***

It seemed as if I had been asleep for hours. My body felt as if it was floating on cloud nine and I didn't feel the throbbing of pain in my temples. I could still smell Jaquellis' cologne and it aroused the fuck out of me. In my head I was in his arms, and I felt as if I truly belonged there. His breath was literally tickling my earlobe and that in turn woke up fat ma. My hand went to my lower lips as I envisioned Jaquellis' hand instead of mine. Strumming my bud, I moaned lowly as I opened my legs wide.

"Quell." I moaned. "Yes, just like that."

Falling onto my back, I paused because my leg landed on something long and hard. The room was pitch black thanks to Cheno installing the blackout curtains I'd requested for my bedroom. My yoni was leaking and I hoped like hell that man wasn't still in my bed, but who else could it have been?

"So, that's the only way I can get you to call me Quell, huh? You getting her ready for me, Honey?"

I could hear the smile that was surely on his face. He was too close for comfort, and I didn't want him to know how embarrassed I truly was. *Live a little, Honey. You don't have to marry the nigga.* Cheno's words echoed in my head, and I smiled. There was no way I could put out the fire I had ignited the way I needed alone. Why not utilize the tool that was lying in my bed after I told his ass to go home hours prior. Jaquellis was about to get a taste of Honey. I just prayed he knew nothing more was happening after this.

"She's ready," I said seductively as I continued massaging my nub.

Jaquellis rubbed my thigh slowly then moved my hand away from my kitty and replaced it with his own. His touch sent a shiver up my spine, and I leaked like a faucet. The only man I'd ever had sex with was Cheese. Anticipation was what I felt in that moment along with a tad bit of fear of allowing another man to enter my sacred place.

"Are you sure you ready for this? There's no turning back."

I nodded but, of course, he couldn't see me agree for him to continue. Instead, I moaned from the friction he caused with his hand. The way he rubbed my pearl was something I'd never experienced, and I loved that shit.

"If we go further, Honey, you will be mine. Is that something you can handle?"

"I. Can. Handle. It." I panted.

At that point I knew I had fucked up because being in a relationship was something I wasn't ready for. The only thing I wanted was for Jaquellis to fuck me long and hard. Had I told him no, he would've gotten up and left, but that shit wasn't going to happen because my pussy was hot and ready like a Little Ceasar's pizza.

He threw the covers to the side and positioned himself between my legs. I didn't expect him to put his mouth on me the first time we got up. Jaquellis had other plans. He was going the whole nine yards; the gloves were off. Rubbing my inner lips with his four fingers at a rapid pace, my bud perked right up for him. Before I knew what was happening, I was wetting up my bed.

"Oooooooouuuuu! Shit!" I came hard as fuck and my back elevated off the mattress.

Jaquellis didn't give me the opportunity to come down from the high I was on. He covered my yoni with his mouth and sucked softly. The sensational feeling crept into my stomach and I was on the verge of releasing my essence once again. I pushed at his forehead but he wasn't budging. His head game was on point, and he had my thighs in a vice grip.

"Oh my God, Quell! What the fuck you doing to me?"

I moaned loudly as I grabbed the back of his head while rotating my mound against his tongue. My movements stilled when he stuck a finger in my ass and an electrical current traveled through my legs. My backdoor always had a *do not enter* sign attached to it. Cheese tried many times to get to that point and failed. For some odd reason, I wanted to take it there with Jaquellis. The way his mouth worked my pearl and his finger assaulted my asshole, a bitch was in a sexual bliss. I bounced on his finger as if it was his manhood while feeding him a full coarse meal.

"Fuck! Fuck! Shit! Okay. Okay." I pled, trying to get him to stop.

"I know you ain't tapping out on me already. I'm not full yet. Now feed me that wet shit, Honey. As a matter of fact…" He got up and I could hear him removing his clothing. Getting back into the bed, he laid next to me and pulled me toward him. "Put that muthafucka in on my face."

Doing as he asked, on wobbly legs, I leveled my sex with his mouth. I must've moved too slowly because he grabbed my thighs and pulled my lower lips onto his mouth. I had to hold on to the headboard so I wouldn't put all of my weight on his face. Rocking, the friction was too much for me to handle. Before long, I was giving his ass a facial and he loved every bit of it and kept going. Jaquellis was devouring fat ma and I could feel her swelling up with every suck of his lips. The nigga was turning my ass out right before my eyes. I came for the fourth time orally and he hadn't even introduced me to the pipe.

"Oh, yeah, she was waiting for that explosion. You can't be holding out on yourself like that. It's not good for the soul," Jaquellis said moving from under me.

My head rested against the headboard with my ass tooted in the air. Jaquellis pulled me down and positioned me on my side. Entering me was like slip and slide because I was so wet. He lifted my leg and filled me up to the tilt. My titties bounced with every stroke and he held on to them with both hands while twisting my nipples. This man didn't know anything about me sexually, but you couldn't tell me that because he did everything correctly.

"Don't stop, Quell. Fuck me harder." I moaned loudly.

He turned my head and kissed me passionately. Our tongues intertwined, never missing a beat. Quell pounded my pussy while kissing me. He lowkey spit in my mouth and I paused mid stroke.

"Did you just spit in my mouth?"

"Mmmhmm. Now come here and give me them lips."

At that point, something inside of me woke up. There were no limits to the things I wanted to do. I turned into a real She Devil and it was probably right up Quell's alley for me to do so. I turned my head once again and kissed him like my life depended on it. That time I wanted him to spit in my mouth because I had just become his nasty bitch. I took hold of his member and guided it to my backdoor.

"You don't have to do that, Honey."

"I know I don't. But I am."

Easing it into my asshole, I winced a little bit because that hole had never been penetrated before. The pain was short lived and turned into pleasure soon after. Quell moaned lowly in my ear as he thrusted deeper. He rubbed my kitty and that made what we were doing so much greater. The combination of him fucking me and massaging my center had me ready to explode. When he started trying to fuck like he was in the coochie, I had to remind him.

"That's not a pussy, Quell. You have to handle that hole with care, or you coming out of that muthafucka."

"My bad; it feels so good. Yo' ass better be ready to say no to these niggas when they approach you. I'm not coming off this shit you just gave me. You belong to me, now."

"Nah, I belong to me. You can come through every now and again." I laughed.

"Oh, that's what you on? Aight, bet."

He flipped me over and instructed me to get on my knees. When I was in position, Quell grabbed both of my wrists and held them behind my back, then he wore the heart of my femineity out. Tears fell from my eyes because he was hitting my spot every time. My face wasn't the only thing that was wet though. My side of the bed was soaked all the way to the foot of it. Fat ma was having the time of her life after a ten-year drought. Quell was staking claim because he sure as hell was putting in work. We went at it for another two hours before I was snoring like a grizzly bear. I'd have to admit, it was the best sleep I had in a long ass time.

I woke up to every part of my body aching. I groaned as I rolled over, and Quell was gone. The way he fucked me kind of had me in my feelings. He could've at least left a note saying he had a good time or something instead of just getting up to leave. I got up and went into the bathroom and turned on the shower. Looking in the mirror, I had hickies on my neck. The shit made me blush like a schoolgirl because I'd never had passion marks left on my body. That alone told me I put it on him real good.

My legs were sore and I didn't hesitate to get in the steamy hot water to soothe the pain. When I cleansed my body with the loofah, my yoni tingled as a flashback entered my mind. I giggled because I was so submissive with Quell and I wondered *is he my Dom now?* To be honest, I wasn't against it. In fact, I wouldn't mind allowing Quell to dominate me sexually. He was a wonderful lover and had me spoiled rotten after one roll in the hay. I couldn't keep my mind off the encounter we shared as I rinsed my body.

Soon as I exited the bathroom with a towel wrapped around my body, my phone rang on the nightstand. When I picked it up, Breeze's picture was on full display. I accepted the call with a smile. "Heyyyyy, Cuzin!" I sang putting the phone on speaker.

"Damn, somebody's happy this morning. I don't need to ask how you doing because you sound great. If I could put my finger on it, I would say you got fucked."

"Now, why would that be the first thing to come out of your mouth? Who would I be having sexual relations with? I'll wait."

Just as I said those words, my bedroom door opened and Quell entered with the same tray he took to the kitchen the night before. The aroma of food hit my nostrils and my stomach growled loudly. My focus was on Quell's tattooed chest and the V-cut that disappeared into his shorts. While I was upset about him leaving, the man was in my kitchen cooking a meal that looked delectable.

"Well, Quell told me he was going to stop by to see how you were doing yesterday. He didn't call to tell me anything, so I assumed you entertained him. Am I wrong?"

"I did come and check on her. She had a headache, and I wouldn't leave until I knew she was better," Quell had the nerve to say.

"Oh, bro, you still there from yesterday? No wonder she is all chipper and shit. You gave her that *dingalang* didn't you?" Breeze laughed. "You finally let a train enter the station. I'm so proud of you, Honey."

I shot Quell a look to be quiet and he chortled as he placed the tray beside me on the bed. He made buttermilk pancakes, cheese eggs, bacon, and hashbrowns. Everything looked great except the bacon was touching the other food.

"Did you make your plate yet?" I asked.

"No, I wanted to make sure you had yours first. What's wrong?"

"I don't eat pork and it's on this plate. You can have this one and I can go fix mine, minus the bacon."

"My bad. I didn't know. I thought because it was in there, that's what you liked."

"Cheno went shopping for me, so anything that is made with pork, won't be eaten by me. I appreciate the fact of you cooking for me though. Thank you."

"I have to go back down and get your fruit and orange juice anyway. Hold tight and I'll be right back." Quell left the room and Breeze was right back on her bullshit.

"He tore yo' ass up, didn't he?"

"Mind ya' business, lil' girl. Now what did you call me for, and how is Cheno doing?" I asked, shutting down the talk of my bedroom extravaganza.

"This ain't over. I'll stay out of it for now, but Cheno is still the same. His vitals are good and we're still playing the waiting game. I called to give you the update on Danica."

"Who the fuck is Danica?"

"Ol' girl that had Cheno's phone. Remember I called and left a voicemail for her to call me about the passcode yesterday."

"Oh, yeah. Did she give it to you?"

"Yup. I've been going through his phone for the past ten minutes. Remember that bitch Charlie beat the fuck up at the block party?"

"What about her?"

"She was the last person to contact Cheno. According to the text messages, she demanded two stacks not to press charges on Charlie. She said she was at the police station on 71st and Cottage. Cheno had to have gotten out of bed to go handle that shit because he didn't want Charlie getting in trouble with the law. It's not a coincidence that he was shot on 71st and Michigan. She texted him saying his time was almost up, but he never texted her back. Instead, he called the bitch. The call lasted less than a minute then she called him back briefly. I think that's when he was t-boned in the intersection. The hoe set him up."

"You got her information, call her ass right now!" I yelled.

"I already did, and the number is out of service. She must've changed her shit. Don't worry though because she's gonna see me. I'm on my way back to the hospital to spend some time with Cheno. I wanted to know if you wanted to come with me."

Quell came back into the room and I licked my lips as I eyeballed him. He moved with such grace, and I knew he'd put some sort of spell on my ass. My thoughts of not being in a relationship went out the window with the way he handled me the night before. There was no way another bitch was going to get the same treatment he'd given me.

"Honey!"

"Huh? What did you say?" I asked dumbfounded.

"Yes, Breeze, she will meet you at the hospital soon as she eats. She has already showered, so give her about an hour to get herself together. I have to go home and get cleaned up myself. I'm meeting up with Fredo a little later, then we can relieve y'all at the hospital."

"Quell, you act like you have to travel hours away." Breeze laughed. "You only live next door."

"Next door!" I screamed.

"Ooops, I gotta go. Honey, I'll see you soon. I love you."

Breeze hung up before I could question her further. I looked at Quell as he tried handing me the tray of food. I didn't take it right away, but the food smelled too good to let it get cold. As I cut the pancakes, buttered them, and then smothered them in syrup, I forked up a couple of triangles and put them in my mouth. The pancakes melted on my tongue.

"Why didn't you tell me you lived next door to me? How did you pull that off?" I asked Quell.

"I didn't choose my crib; Cheno did. You never asked where I lived so I didn't think to tell you. If I remember correctly, you only asked was I staying in a hotel downtown and I told you no. I also said I was in the process of moving into my home."

"Well, you could've told me you lived on the other side of the fence. After what we did last night, how am I supposed to get away from the dick assault you put on me?"

"Honey, you don't have to get away from anything. I told you once we went all the way you belonged to me. And I meant that shit. Conformed that coochie to react to me and only me. Plus, I took your booty virginity. You gon' love me forever for that deed alone."

"Sounds good. Don't push your luck. Eat your food so you can go across the way and wash your ass."

Quell laughed as he chewed the hashbrowns he had in his mouth. "If I wanted to, I could get in the shower right here and have yo' ass bent over in there with me. But since you already made plans to meet up with Breeze, you safe…for now. I can't promise nothing won't happen later. I may need to give your mean ass another dose."

"Whatever. It wasn't all you make it out to be," I said rolling my eyes at him.

"Shid, you lying. The way you were cumming all over my face and throwing that ass back told me all I needed to know. If you can fake orgasms like that, you good. I truly believe I got the real deal out of you, Shawty, and that was only a taste. There's more where that came from. You thought you were screaming my name so the neighborhood knows who that pussy belongs to. My pipe print gon' be permanently etched in yo' stomach next go round."

I had to squeeze my legs together because he was turning me on with every word he spoke. It was in my best interest to keep my mouth closed, so I chose to eat instead. My face heated up because I could feel him watching my every move and that alone had me on the verge of wetting the bed. After finishing my meal, I drank the last of my juice and stood to leave the room.

Quell beat me to the door and took the tray from me. "Get dressed, beautiful. I got this. Once I wash the dishes, I'm heading out. Call me if you need me," he said kissing my forehead.

"I don't have your number, Quell."

"It's in your phone." He smirked then turned to walk away. Stopping in his tracks he said, "Don't ever try to play on my top, Honey. I spelled my name in that shit; that's why you no longer have the desire to call me Jaquellis. The name is Quell, baby. That's the nigga that's in charge of your heart from this day forward. I'll see you later." He winked leaving the room.

I couldn't think of a comeback because his ass was correct. The only name on my mind was Quell and he was the muthafuckin' man around these parts.

Chapter 5

Fredo

Imagine life, at its full peak
Then imagine, lying dead, in the arms of your enemy
Imagine peace on this earth, when there's no grief
Imagine grief on this earth, when there's no peace
Everybody's got a different way of endin' it
And when your number comes for service then they send
it in
Now your time has arrived for your final test
I see fear in your eyes and hear your final breath

For the first time in my life, I had to turn off Scarface's song *I Seen a Man Die* because thinking of my nigga not pulling through this shit was killing me from the inside out. When I walked into the hospital room seeing Cheno lying in that bed motionless, my knees buckled. There was no way in hell my nigga was caught slipping and got wet up like that. I was out for blood, but the streets weren't talking. It was time to take the shit up a notch because revenge was the only thing on my mind and that muthafucka named Free was on the top of my list.

His ass been missing in action since the trap was hit and that wasn't like him at all. I went to his crib, and it seemed like he hadn't been there in a hot minute. Shid, I even went to his OG's crib and she swore on the bible she hadn't heard from him either. She was crying as if the nigga was dead, but I knew better. Tina was the type of mama that would protect her kids through hell and high waters, so I didn't believe her far as I could spit. She always knew where Free was at all times.

Cruising down the Nine, I was heading to the trap to make sure everything was running smoothly. Plus, I was meeting up with Quell. Breeze wanted to shut everything down until further notice, but I wasn't having that shit. Being Cheno's righthand man, it was my job to make sure his organization ran just as smoothly as it did if he was on vacation and I was in charge.

I may not be a Chicagoan by nature, but when my nigga said he needed me, I was on the first thing smoking. Cheno had everything on lock down south, and he still had his hand in the cookie jar. But the shit he had going on in the Chi was on a whole other level. We rose to the occasion and made a name for ourselves out in these streets and things were going well until somebody decided to be greedy.

Cheno took care of everybody on his team, and these muthafuckas was biting the hand that fed their ass. The fact that he was laid up, unresponsive, in a coma pissed me off. I'd been fuckin' my brain cells up trying to figure all this shit out and nothing was clicking. The only muthafuckas I knew were on the shit list was Cheese, his muthafuckin' robbing ass cousin, and Free's janky ass.

When I pulled up to the trap, niggas were on point just like they were supposed to be. I got out of my whip and the fiends were out and about like zombies. Business was looking good, and I knew there was nothing to worry about at the moment. Lil' Mike walked up the street toward me. I waited for him to make a sale then he came up to me and we dapped each other up.

"How's things going?" I asked pulling a cigarette from behind my ear, lighting it.

"We straight. Money's flowing through this bitch like spring water down a stream. But I need to holla at you about something."

"What's up?" I asked taking a pull off my cig.

"At the block party, I told Cheno I knew that bitch Larisa from somewhere. I couldn't pinpoint where I remembered her from, but it came to me last night after you told me what happened to him. She used to fuck with a nigga named Lord from out west. Lord works for Cheese and it's not a coincidence that his ex was fighting Charlie because of Cheno."

"So, do you think she had a hand in what happened to him?"

"It's possible. I'm trying to cover all bases because whoever did the homie like that got to pay for that shit." Lil' Mike paced in front of me with his fist balled tight. "Free is getting his muthafuckin' ass whooped when I see him because the nigga moving foul. Where is he?"

"Nobody has seen him. Rest assured though, his ass will be dealt with accordingly," I said plucking my cigarette butt into the street. "What else do you have on that Larisa bitch?"

"I gave you all the information I know. There's nothing else I got for you, but my ears will stay glued to the streets. Another thing, Sketty was supposed to be here today but he's a no call no show."

Just as Lil' Mike said his name, Sketty pulled up in his Impala and jumped out quickly. I glared at his ass because he was late as hell and I couldn't wait to hear the excuse he had for me. Sketty was handpicked by Cheno and I didn't like him from the first day of meeting him. Something was off with the nigga, but I couldn't put my finger on it.

"What's up, Fredo? Sorry I'm late. I had to take my granny to the emergency room because her sugar levels were high as fuck. I heard about Cheno and that shit fucked up. Any word on who did that shit?"

I looked at Sketty as if he had three muthafuckin' heads because he was talking too fuckin' fast for my liking. His eyes were shifty, and he never looked in my direction. That alone told me he was talking at me and not to me. I didn't respect shit like that because the shit was shiesty as fuck.

"Nawl, we don't know what the fuck going on with that. But my question to is, what the fuck have *you* found out?" I asked. When Sketty continued to avoid eye contact, I yoked his ass up and forced him to look me in the eye like a man. "What the fuck did you find out, nigga?"

"Fredo, the last I heard was Cheno didn't make it. Is that true?"

"Nigga—"

"I got this, Lil' Mike." I sneered at him. "Nigga, you heard right. My brother is gone and the muthafuckas behind his death is going to pay out the ass soon as I find out who's behind it. The way yo' punk ass all jittery and shit got me thinking you know more than you saying. Get yo' suspect ass the fuck from around here before I put a bullet in yo' muthafuckin' head!"

Shoving Sketty away from me, he hurried to his car without another word. I saw Quell about to park and pulled out my phone. He answered right away.

"You good?"

"Follow that muthafuka in that Impala and tell me every muthafuckin' move he makes," I barked in his ear. "Lil' Mike, jump in that truck with Quell."

Lil' Mike jumped in and they took off behind Sketty.

"When y'all find out what he's on, hit my line, ASAP. That nigga on some dummy shit and I got a bullet with his name on it. The only people that know Cheno is still alive out of the crew is the three of us and his family. Keep it that way. Long as the streets thinks he's dead, my nigga safe. I'm about to do my own research and we'll meet up later."

"Bet," Quell said ending the call.

I went into the trap and grabbed the money from the week of sales and bounced. I thought back to the day of the block party and who that bitch Larisa was with. From memory I remembered three of the hoes, but I wasn't into beating on females. I needed Breeze and Honey in on this shit with me. Honey was fresh out of the pen, and I really didn't want to involve her in this street shit. At the stoplight I grabbed my phone and hit Breeze up.

"Fredo, what's good?"

"Aye, where you at? I need you to ride with me."

"I'm at the hospital with Cheno. What's going on?"

"I want to go check out the bitch Charlie beat the fuck out of at the block party. Lil' Mike said she fucked with some nigga named Lord that works for Cheese. I think she set bro up to get hit."

"And I'm here to say you on the right track. Where you wanna meet, because Charlie just got here, and me and Honey was about to go on a scavenger hunt to find the hoe ourselves. I'll fill you in on what I found out when I get with you."

"You knew this already?" I asked astoundingly.

"Yup. Found out this morning when I accessed Cheno's phone. Where we meeting, Fredo? As a matter of fact, meet me on 70th and St. Lawrence. We leaving the hospital now."

"What the fuck over there?"

"Sia's crib. The bitch knows Larisa and she gon' tell me what the fuck I want to know or else."

Breeze hung up and I hightailed it down the Nine headed eastbound. I kept saying the name Sia over and over until it clicked who she was. She was Breeze's little girlfriend but I didn't know why Sia would be involved with a bitch that set up her girl's brother. Then I remembered that Breeze kicked her to the curb for Taz's fine ass. There was definitely some animosity there for Sia to want some get back against Breeze. I only hoped she knew what the fuck she got herself into because Breeze didn't play about Cheno.

Ten minutes later, I parked on the block and called to see what Breeze's estimated time of arrival would be. She picked up and said she was pulling up and banged on me. Not even two minutes went by when Breeze pulled up to the passenger side of my whip. I rolled the window down so I could hear what she had to say.

"Follow me to the middle of the block," she said then pulled off.

Doing as I was instructed, Breeze parked her Camero on the left side of the street in front of a three-story building, and I found a spot a couple spaces up. As I got out my whip, she jumped out with Honey right behind her. I had to jog to catch up to them because Breeze was on a muthafuckin' mission. She wasn't messing around. When we got to the door, Breeze fumbled with her keyring then inserted a key into the lock.

"You still got a key to the bitch crib?"

"When a muthafucka hope and pray you gon' forgive them for the bullshit they did, they'll leave the door open for you to walk right in. Unfortunately for her, I'm coming in regardless."

Breeze unlocked the outer door and skipped up the steps to the second floor. She inserted another key into the keyhole and pushed the door open as if she lived there followed by Honey. I closed the door behind me, and Breeze walked further into the apartment and went into a room off the kitchen.

"Get the fuck up, Sia!" she yelled.

"Breeze, what are you doing here so early?"

"Put some clothes on and meet me in the living room. Not now, but *right* now."

Walking back out where me and Honey were, Breeze was breathing heavily. There was no way Sia was about to hold out on anything Breeze wanted to know because she was going to get the worse ass whooping she ever received in life if she did. Breeze looked the same way Cheno did when he was about to handle business, and I was ready to see how she handled her shit. If it was anything like that nigga, the shit was about to be gruesome.

Sia walked out of the room with a pair of shorts and a t-shirt on. Her hair was wrapped in a silk scarf, and she was rubbing the hell out of her eyes. "Breeze, why the fuck you got these muthafuckas in my house?"

"That's the least of your worries, Sia. Have a seat."

"For what?" she snapped.

"I'm asking the questions from this point on. I'm not gon' repeat myself again. Sit. The. Fuck. Down!"

Sia remained standing and that only infuriated Breeze more. In two strides she was across the room with her hand wrapped around Sia's throat. She picked Sia off her feet and slung her on the couch, causing her to bounce off, hitting her head on the corner of the coffee table.

"What the hell is your problem?" Sia asked, struggling to get up.

"Who the fuck is Larisa and where can I find her?"

Sia stood with the look of a deer caught in headlights. She backed away from Breeze but didn't get too far before she was pulled back by the front of her shirt. Yanking out of the hold Breeze had on her, Sia turned to walk away. Why the fuck did she do that shit?

Breeze gripped the back of her neck like she was a dog owner then rammed her face right into the nearest wall. "Bitch, where is Larisa? She's yo' muthafuckin' friend and I need to holla at her!"

Sia had her hand over her nose with blood dripping between her fingers.

"I told you I wasn't going to be repeating myself, and here I am doing just that. Answer me before I fuck you up!"

"I don't know where she's at."

Breeze punched her in the mouth, followed by a blow to the side of her head. "Lie again! Where do the bitch live, Sia? I know you don't want to be found in this muthafucka stankin'. That bitch had my brother setup and she's going to pay for that shit with her life."

"She left—"

Breeze hit her again and that time I heard her jaw crack. The shit made me cringe because it only took one solid punch. Cheno style. Sia was leaking on the hardwood floor, and I moved to grab Breeze away from her.

"Don't touch me!" She gritted before turning her attention back to Sia. "I don't give a damn if you have to tell me what I want to know through yo' muthafuckin' nose, I want an address on Larisa, and I want it now!" Breeze reached behind her back and brought her Nine out and cocked it.

Sia started crying loudly with her hands up to protect herself. There was no way she was going to block a bullet, but I bet she was going to try. Breeze had the look of death in her eyes and she wasn't backing down.

Sia coughed and blood flew from her mouth. "Please, don't kill me. I love you so much, Breeze," she mumbled. "I'll tell you where she is."

"Get to talking, then. I don't have all fucking day!"

"She lives out west on 15th and Trumbull. The address is 1529 S. Trumbull Avenue. It's a white building, and she lives on the first floor. Larisa lives with her boyfriend named Lord." Sia paused to catch her breathe. She wiped her mouth with the back of her hand. "Breeze, I swear I didn't know she was fucking with Cheno for Cheese."

"So, Cheese put her up to going after my cousin?" Honey asked. Sia nodded and Honey punched her ass in the eye. "Bitch, you claim to love my little cousin and you didn't think to tell her those muthafuckas were plotting on her brother!"

"I didn't know!" Sia cried.

"How the hell you didn't know and you just ran the shit down a minute ago? Bitch, you just as guilty as the nigga that pulled the trigga. You simple ass hoes gon' learn these niggas only used yo' dumb ass to do what they couldn't, and you and Larisa fell for the bait. I hope you enjoyed whatever the fuck they gave you to keep that secret because you gon' take that shit to the grave. Kill that bitch so we can get the fuck up outta here."

In a blink of an eye, Sia's brains splattered against the eggshell white wall. I didn't even notice when Breeze screwed the damn silencer on the gun. A tear fell from Breeze's eye, but she wiped it away as she went into the room Sia came out of. She came out with a towel in hand, and she started wiping down everything she touched. After she was sure to get rid of any evidence, she took her phone out.

"What up, Perk. I got a water leak at 7021 S. St. Lawrence; second floor. Come through the back. There's a lot of water so you gon' need a wet vac, pronto." Breeze headed for the door while pocketing her phone, "Let's get the fuck outta here. I need to get something to eat before we get out west to handle this other bitch."

***

We ended up going to Valois on 53rd because Breeze wanted breakfast. We sat at a table in the far corner of the restaurant so we could talk without being heard. Honey sat silently scrolling through her phone as Breeze told me everything she found out in Cheno's phone. Hearing that shit made me mad as hell and I was ready to gather up the troops to handle these niggas.

My phone vibrated and I hurriedly took it from my pocket; it was Quell. "Talk to me."

"This nigga Sketty is over here on 15th and Trumbull. There's a gang of niggas gathered around listening to whatever he is saying." Quell paused for a second then Lil' Mike's voice came through on the line.

"Fredo, the bitch I was telling you about is with these niggas. Larisa. Sketty is real chummy with these muthafuckas, and I believe we got the mole in our group. What you want us to do?"

"Get the fuck out of there. Take pics so we'll be able to identify them niggas then bounce because y'all won't get out of there alive with it just being two of y'all. I bet that nigga went right over there and told them Cheno was dead. Exactly what I wanted him to do. I knew something wasn't right with that pussy muthafucka. We gotta come up with a plan before they formulate an attack first. Meet us at the hospital."

"We need a lot of shooters on our team because these niggas deep," Lil' Mike said.

"Don't worry about it. We gon' be straight. Do what needs to be done and get out of there. Keep ya' head on the swivel."

Quell ended the call and the only thing I could do was shake my head. The waitress came over with me and Breeze's food. Honey ordered a strawberry shake with whipped cream and a cherry. She wasn't hungry because she had a big breakfast before she left the house. Honey was in her phone tough and the shit had me curious to what she was doing.

"What you got going on over there, Honey?"

"I'm checking Cheese's social media to see what he's up to." She replied without looking up. "I haven't seen much on his page, *but* his bitch is another story. That's what's wrong with these hoes. They talk too fuckin' much. Putting all their business on that blue app. Now she gon' wish she hadn't because I'm on her ass. Letty and Cheese gon' be at the basketball tournament in Douglas Park this afternoon. You wanna go, Breeze?"

I cut in. "Nah, shit too fuckin' hot right now. The last thing I need is for something to happen to one of y'all. Let me set this play up then we will go at all them muthafuckas. Until then, I need y'all to lay low."

"Fredo is right, cuz. That bitch's day is coming, and you will be able to swell her shit up like a pumpkin. I just want to go sit with my brother for the time being anyway. Killing Sia did something to me. That bitch twat was fire."

I laughed loud as hell because out of all things Breeze could say about what happened, she was talking about Sia's dead ass box. Yeah, her and Cheno had the same DNA for sure. I finished eating my food and reached in my pocket to pay the tab. Breeze threw a bill on the table and stood.

"Man, if you don't get yo' ass outta here with that bullshit. You know muthafuckin' well I'm not about to sit up here and let you pay for my food. Put that shit back in yo' pocket. I got it."

"You ain't said shit but a word," Breeze said, snatching her money off the table. "I'll race you to the hospital. If I beat you there, I need five hunnid." She smirked.

"I got too much money in my whip to be getting stopped by the pigs fuckin' with you. As a matter of fact, I need to put that shit in yo' trunk so you can take it and put it where it belongs."

"Say less."

Breeze walked out of the restaurant and I followed behind Honey. The way they were whispering as they walked to the parking lot, I knew they were on pure bullshit, but I wasn't gon' say a word. I would be there to handle what they couldn't, though. And that was on my muthafuckin' brother.

Chapter 6

Charlie

"Come on, Cheno, you have to come out of this. Shit is crazy out here without you. I would be satisfied to argue with you one more time just to hear your voice. I'm all cried out. Actually, I know you don't want to hear about all my sadness."

Cheno still hadn't moved a muscle and it was getting harder to sit and watch him in the condition he was in. When Breeze left, I took it upon myself to wash his face then gave him a sponge bath. I even brushed his hair. If I could, I would've given him a haircut while I was at it. I oiled him up with Shea butter, and if he was able, Cheno would've cursed and screamed because he hated the smell of it.

There was a light knock on the door before it opened. A nurse walked in with a bathtub. "Hello, how's Mr. Brown today?"

"He's the same."

"I'm going to check his vitals and IV bag, then get him cleaned up."

"You can check is vitals and all that other shit, but I've already cleaned him up. That would be my job for the duration of his stay. Please, pass the word. Thank you."

The smile on the nurse's face dropped immediately. She did what she had to do and left soon after. Before the door could close completely, Breeze walked in with Honey, Fredo, Quell, and Lil' Mike. The hospital staff decided

Cheno could have unlimited visitors after being cursed out on numerous occasions.

Lil' Mike walked over to the bed and bowed his head while looking at Cheno. He wiped a hand down his face then pat his boss on the shoulder. Honey and Quell were eyeing each other and I knew right off the bat something was going on between them. I was about to call them out on it, but Quell's voice deterred my attention to him.

"Breeze, you never told me what you found in Cheno's phone."

My ears perked up.

"The night Cheno was shot; he was texting with Larisa." Breeze looked over at me. "She told him she wanted two thousand dollars to not go to the police on Charlie. She was supposedly outside of the police station and sent a photo to prove herself. Larisa said he didn't give a damn about his bitch when Cheno said he wasn't giving her shit."

I chuckled.

"Charlie, don't do that," Breeze said angrily. "From the looks of it, my brother was out in the wee hours of the morning to protect you! Larisa was at the police station on 71st and Cottage. Cheno was shot on 71st and Michigan; do the muthafuckin' math."

"So, she set him up?" I asked sitting up in the chair.

"Hell yeah, she did!" Lil' Mike replied. "That explains why she was over there with them niggas in Cheese crew."

"What we gon' do about it?"

"Charlie, like I told Breeze, shit is hot right now. Nobody ain't doing shit until I give the go ahead. Cheno getting better should be our main focus for the time being. As of now, Cheno is dead. That's what we're going with for now. The only people that know he's still alive are the people in his direct circle," Fredo said looking around the room.

"If word gets out that Cheno is still breathing, the muthafuckas will come back to finish the job. Charlie, I need you to man his businesses, and I have the traps on lock. I've already collected his money and turned it over to Breeze. This is what needs to be done until we can figure out what to do next. In other words, live ya' life normal as possible and don't draw attention to yourselves."

"I need time out of this hospital. Who is up to stay with Cheno tonight? I want to go out."

It was Friday and I needed to think about what I wanted to do about Larisa. The ass whooping I gave her only made the bitch do the unthinkable and she crossed the muthafuckin' line. Cheno wasn't in a position to help her funky ass whenever I got my claws in her. At my big age, fighting wasn't something I was proud of doing. But whatever it took, I was willing to do because I was tired of the hoe that couldn't understand the type of nigga Cheno was.

He cheated throughout our relationship and kept that shit on the low until he couldn't. I should have walked away when he showed me the first time, but I didn't. My downfall was forgiving him time after time. The day I decide to walk away from the bullshit, Cheno got hurt and it was behind a bitch that once had his cum on her tongue. One would say fuck her and for me to leave the situation alone. Nah, Larisa is going to learn to keep her hands off shit that doesn't belong to her.

"I can stay with Big Homie," Lil' Mike spoke up.

"Cool. I'll be back tomorrow. For now, I'm going home to sleep in my bed," I said gathering my things. I walked across the room and stopped in front of Breeze. "I'll call you when I wake up."

Leaving the room, I went to the elevator with a lot on my mind. When I stepped out of the automatic doors, the heat smacked me in my face forcing me to make a beeline to my vehicle. As I sat in the smothering hot car, I turned the air conditioning on full blast then lowered the window. After a while, I pulled off toward the expressway. The last conversation with Cheno played in my head for the umpteenth time and I tried my best to shake it off. I was feeling guilty for the words I said, but at the time he needed to hear that shit.

The commute to Cheno's house wasn't as bad as I thought it would be. I pulled into his driveway and made my way inside. I'd been staying in the home I used to share with Cheno for the past couple days. His scent could be smelled throughout every room. As bad as I wanted to forgive him for his infidelities, I just couldn't get over the fact of him playing in my face with these money-hungry bitches. Maybe if he hadn't stuck his dick in them…nah, I'm lying. He shouldn't have given any of them hoes the time of day when he had a woman who did any and everything for his ass. Why commit to me then go seek another muthafucka for whatever type of gratification?

That was a conversation for Cheno and me to have when the moment presented itself. Until then, it was on me to get back at the bitch involved in his near-death experience. I may not like Cheno right now, but my loyalty will forever be with that man. Whether we're together as a couple or not, I'm gonna have his back regardless. Some may call me stupid. Others may stress how dumb I was, but I didn't give a fuck what anyone said. Cheno had been there for me when nobody else was and I'm riding for him in his absence.

Climbing the stairs to the second level, I went straight to the bathroom to shower. The smell of the hospital was the scent in my nostrils, and I wanted to rid myself of that. It was a different atmosphere without Cheno being in the home and the silence was smothering me. After showering, I put on one of his shirts and crawled in bed. My phone woke me up hours later and it was dark as hell outside. Feeling underneath the pillows for my phone, I finally located it just in time to answer.

"Hello." I croaked out.

"Damn, you sound like yo' breath stank!" Breeze laughed.

"Fuck you! What you want, man?"

"I've been waiting on you to call me when you woke up. Obviously, if I hadn't called, you'd still be slobbing. Where you at?"

"At Cheno's." I responded sitting up.

"For a bitch that quit him, you shole is running up his electricity. I'll be there in a minute."

"You got jokes, hoe. This will forever be my place of peace. I won't even go into explaining this shit to you, Breeze. You wouldn't even begin to understand. And why are you coming here?"

"Stop playing with me. You got some shit you need to get off your chest and I'm coming to you just in case I have to bust yo' face open."

"You don't want no smoke." I laughed. "I'm here whenever you decide to come through."

Breeze hung up, forcing me to get up. I glanced at the time and it was seven-thirty. I hadn't planned to sleep long as I did. However, I guess my body needed the rest. Going into the bathroom to handle my hygiene, I jumped in the shower again because my skin felt clammy. Soon as I got out and wrapped the towel around my body, Breeze was screaming through the house like a mad woman.

Hurrying to dry off before she made her way to the bedroom, her girl-liking ass busted through the door without knocking. "Damn! All that ass right there! I know damn well my brother wasn't fuckin' around and he had all that in this house!"

I turned around fast as hell while snatching the sheet from the bed to cover myself. Glaring at Breeze through slits, if looks could kill, her ass would've been laid out in the doorway. She knew not to play with me like that.

"Go find something safe to do, Breeze." I rolled my eyes. "I'll be down once I get dressed."

"Why you mad at me because you got a wagon that you draggin' sitting on yo' back? I'm just shocked Cheno fumbled the play on that shit. The Larisa chick ain't got nothing on you. Maybe you should come to the dark—"

"Breeze, get the fuck out!"

"Okay. Don't bite my head off. I'm going." She laughed, closing the door behind her.

Breeze was a muthafucka you had to love to hate. She kept me out of jail plenty of times behind her brother and I loved her to death. I knew she meant no harm with the things she said, but the shit was irritating at times. I threw on some joggers and a wife beater before going downstairs.

"Where you at, hoe?" I yelled.

"In the kitchen."

"Your ass stay eating and don't gain a pound," I said taking a seat at the island.

"You want me to introduce you to the weed diet? It works for me." She cackled. "All you gotta do is smoke, eat, smoke, eat, smoke, smoke, smoke, and eat again. Oh wait, then smoke."

I laughed hard as hell because that was just about what her nutty ass did daily. I'll pass. There is nothing healthy about smoking all fucking day. Breeze hadn't changed from the first time Cheno introduced me to her and I didn't see her doing so anytime soon.

"So, what were you going to call me about?" she asked, biting into a Hot Pocket.

"Nothing important. I want to go out. Let's hit up G-Spot and have fun. I need to get my mind off Cheno for a couple hours."

"We can do that," Breeze said tapping away on her phone.

"Who you texting?" I asked being nosy.

"We going in that bitch deep. Ain't no more rolling solo. Niggas out here plotting and I'd be damned if they catch us without warning. I hate we can't just go through their shit and light that bitch up like a Christmas tree. Time will present itself though and I can't wait to put in work with

Cheno's AR-15. He ain't here to stop me from making his baby sing either."

My phone pinged at the same time as Breeze's. She must've started a group text because messages were coming in by the boatload. Everybody in the crew responded and was down to go out with us. We hadn't been out together as a unit since Honey's welcome home party. We agreed to meet at the club about ten-thirty. Breeze put her phone on the counter and zoned out on me.

"What's wrong, sis? One minute you're excited about busting a gun, then you go silent. Speak your mind."

Shaking her head, Breeze wiped what I assumed were tears from her eyes. It was the second time I'd seen her cry and I felt bad for her. Something other than Cheno getting shot was eating her up. I hoped she would open up to me about it. And she did after a couple minutes.

"Man, Charlie…" Her voice trailed off for a second while she blew out a deep breath. "This wasn't my first, second, nor third body. Hell, I'm true to this shit. Sia. Sia was different. Why the didn't she just give the bitch up? I would've let her ass make it."

Breeze laughed in the mist of crying. That was when I knew she had the blood of Cheno running through her veins. He could go from hot to cold in a millisecond. His sister was no different.

"The lie I just told sounded good. Sia had to go off the strength of her association with Larisa. Sia not coming to me about my brother was an added bonus. As much love I had for her ass, it held no weight to the fact she showed me what type of muthafucka she really was. It will forever be bros before hoes. No matter who the bitch was."

"You really killed that girl, Breeze?"

Her eyebrow rose as she stared at me. "You thought I didn't? She knew more than she was willing to tell. My brother could be dead and her funky ass made the decision to go mute about the situation. So, I silenced her for life."

Like I knew she would, Breeze pulled a blunt from her pocket and flamed up. The way she held the smoke in, one would've thought her lungs were screaming for oxygen. Soon as she released the smoke, I got an instant contact. I smoked but not on the level as Breeze. Her ass was always on demon time with it. No longer wanting to talk about the murder she had committed, I changed the subject.

"I done told y'all to come out and I don't even have anything to wear. I'm gonna have to meet y'all at the club because I have to drive out to Downers Grove to get dressed."

"Downers Grove? Why the fuck you go all the way out there, Charlie?"

"I wanted to be far away from Cheno and the drama. I needed time to myself to think about what I really wanted to do when it came to me and your brother. Being away from him was all I was thinking about. I chose me and I don't regret it. The place I'm staying is temporary until I find a more permanent place to live."

Breeze blew out a cloud of smoke. "What you gon' do when Cheno is released from the hospital? He will be coming home. Are you going to be there to help him until he's better?"

I thought about what Breeze asked and I had every intention of being there to nurse Cheno back to health. When I say my loyalty is forever, that's what the fuck I meant. There was no way I was going to leave Cheno to fend for himself during his recovery. Regardless of what we've been through, Cheno was my best friend.

"No doubt. I will be there long as he needs me. After that, it's a wrap. Me and Cheno is done and over with, Breeze. One day I may be able to forgive him for doing me dirty. Until then, friendship is all I see us maintaining from this point on. Cheno will be able to fuck around with whomever he chooses without having to worry about hurting me, his business coming back to me, or hearing my mouth."

"Yeah, aight." She chuckled. "We can go make a mall run real quick so you won't have to drive damn near an hour to Downers Grove and then the thirty or so minutes to the club. We have a little time to spare and still make it to the club at the meet up time."

"I'm down with that. Let me go put on my shoes then I'll be ready." I left Breeze sitting while enjoying her weed and went upstairs. She had given me something else to think about and I had to process it. I would face the task of taking care of Cheno whenever he opened his eyes and walked out of that hospital.

Chapter 7

Honey

I'd been stalking Cheese's social media since Lil' Mike revealed one of his workers were responsible for what happened to Cheno. Cheese hadn't tried to contact me and I was grateful he stayed away from me. The thought of him wanting my cousin dead did something to me and I was trying to conjure up a plan to get close to him. I was keeping my thoughts to myself because I knew Fredo, and especially Quell, would be against what I wanted to do.

My phone was in my hand when I received a message from Breeze. They wanted to go out and I was all in with the plan. With so much shit going on, we needed this time to drink and have fun. It kind of worried me that no one tried to come for the rest of Cheno's crew. I guess this was the quiet before the storm and they were plotting the same way I was. Only time would tell though and there was nothing for any of us to do except watch our backs and stay alert.

As I rummaged through my closet for something to wear for the night, I thought about my mama. I'd been out of prison over two months and she hadn't even sent a smoke signal to me. I didn't even know why it surprised me because not one time did she visit me in jail. One day soon I was going to pay her a visit so we could talk about the beef she had with her one and only child. Nothing would ever make me believe my own mama hated me over a nigga. I would find out soon enough. I was going to make it my business to go there as an adult. Not as a seventeen-year-old child.

Destinee Lynn's *Feenin'* started playing and my mind went back to the sex session I had with Quell. That man had me twisted like a pretzel and molded my pussy to only want what he was offering. Some of the shit we did behind closed doors were the nastiest I'd ever been with a muthafucka. Cheese ain't never took me to the level Quell had me on. It was hard as hell not to take his chocolate ass into the bathroom at the hospital for a quickie. But I had to behave because it wasn't the time nor the place.

I decided to wear an olive-green maxi dress which crisscrossed over my breasts, and matching stilettos. Throwing the dress on the bed, I plugged my flat irons in, placing them on the vanity. My phone pinged. When I looked to see who had texted me, I smiled bigger than Nelly when he got Ashanti back.

Quell: Hey, I was just checking on you. What you got going on?

Me: I'm getting ready to shower. I'm going out with the girls tonight.

Quell: I want you to have a good time. Watch yo' surroundings, Honey. Call me if you need me.

Me: Will do. ttyl

I wanted to tell him so bad that I would rather spend the night with him, but I wouldn't hear the end of it if I ditched my girls for dick. Walking into the bathroom, I started the shower to get the water at the temperature I needed. I swayed to the music while cleansing my face. It felt so good to be in the comfort of my own home. Being a woman coming from the prison system, it was hard to adjust to the outside world. My business was what kept me grounded, and now I've added Quell to the mix.

Everything going on with Cheno threw a monkey wrench into the game and I could picture myself going back into the system. I was waiting on something to pop off because what happened to the one man who held me down while I was in prison wasn't cool. I owed Cheno my life and I was going to put it on the line for him. Cheese was siding with his cousin instead of turning his ass in for what was done. He was guilty too and would go down, right along with Tank. There was no way he could say he knew nothing about what went on. Everybody involved was going to get touched. I didn't give a fuck what happens at that point.

Pulling the shower cap over my hair, I stepped into the shower and almost melted under the stream of the hot water. Chris Brown's *Sensational* came through the speaker of my phone and I started a whole song and dance in the shower. I loved his music so much. It always got me in the mood to get through my day.

Sensational. What can I do for you, girl.
And I know, and I know, and I know, girl
I act fool for you
Loves like a riddle, yeah
Give me the clues solve a riddle
Oh, ah. Laugh just a little, yeah
Life's pretty sweet, can't be bitter
She tell me love her 'til the morning na-na-na

I was having a good time in the shower. Taking my sweet time. This type of thing happened every time I showered because there wasn't a time period of how long I could be in there. After three songs, I got out because the water was warming up on me. I moisturized my body and put my robe on before walking back into my room. Sitting at my vanity, I parted my hair in sections to get ready for the night. It was almost nine o'clock and I had to get a move on.

Finally finishing my hair, I had it bone straight with a part down the middle. I applied nude makeup and was ready to go. Sending a message in the group text, I let them know I was heading out. Breeze was on her way and the others hadn't responded. I changed purses and put my phone and gun inside along with my wallet. I looked around to make sure I wasn't leaving anything behind then turned off the lights in my bedroom.

Going into the garage after setting the alarm, I was ready to hit the streets. I jumped into my truck and the first thing I did after starting it up was turned the air on full blast. It was hot as hell, even at the late hour and I hated that shit. But the weather was not going to stop me from having a good time. I backed out and waited for the garage door to lower before I continued backing into the street. My phone was going off like crazy, causing me to pause to see what was going on.

Breeze: Me and Taz heading to the club.

Charlie: I'm leaving out now.

Spanky: I'm here and it's packed. Y'all have to park in the lot across the street.

Tiny: Cool because I was circling the block trying to find a space. I'm headed that way now Spanky.

Goldie: I got Tequila with me, and we'll be there in five.

Breeze: Honey, where you at?

I was stopped at a red light and I replied quickly. *Just leaving the house. I'll be there fast as traffic allows. Somebody stay in the lot and save me a spot.*

Breeze: I'll pay for you and save you a spot next to me. Just get here.

Honey: Thanks, cuz. I'm on the way.

A horn blared behind me, prompting me to move forward. I scrolled through my Apple playlists until I found the one I wanted to listen to. Vibing all the way to the club, traffic was on my side because I was rolling smoothly. I ate that expressway up and the GPS guided me to the lot where Breeze was waiting patiently for me.

"What you do, fly here?" she asked laughing once the attendant allowed me entry.

"No, the expressway was clear, and I took that shit for what it was." I hit the lock button on my key fob. "What's up with this club? It seems like a popular one."

"It is. A nigga named G opened this place a few years ago and the shit been hittin' ever since. G-Spot is the place to be when you want to have a good time. There is no drama allowed either."

"That's what I'm talking about. Let's party then!"

We made our way across the street and walked right up to the door. There were a few murmurs from the hoes that were standing in line, but Breeze ignored the fuck out of them. She whispered in the ear of one of the guys doing security then dapped him up. The nigga looked me up and down, licking his lips. Wasn't shit happening, but I didn't have to voice that.

"She's off limits, fam. That's your cousin Honey."

"Damn. That's why it's important for the family to get together more often," he said shaking his head. "Soon as shit dies down out here, I'll be in to kick it with y'all. Nikki is in there somewhere with Shon and Cleve."

"Bet," Breeze said as we walked inside.

She led the way to the VIP section she was able to get for us and it was lit. All our girls were already having a time with drinks flowing. I needed something to eat so I picked up a menu to place an order. I chose a plate of garlic parmesan wings, fries, and chicken quesadillas. A bottle girl came through right on time and took my order. Before she could leave, I asked if anyone else wanted anything and they didn't. I didn't give a damn. More for me.

The DJ was spinning the tunes and once again I was introduced to artists I hadn't known about. For some odd reason it felt as if somebody was watching me. Looking around, I couldn't pinpoint where the individual was and it only caused me to pay attention to my surroundings. Waiting on my food, I got up and danced a little bit with Tiny because there was no way I was drinking on an empty stomach.

My food arrived and I spent the next twenty minutes getting my eat on. I finished every morsel and didn't regret it one bit. I chased it all down with a bottled water before filling a cup with tequila and pineapple juice to join the party that was going on without me. Two-stepping to the music, I noticed a group of females and a man walking up the stairs to our section. They walked right over to Breeze, so I didn't pay it much attention until they started walking in my direction.

"Honey, I want you to meet your cousins Keyshae', Nikki, Shon, and Cleve. These are just a few of them," Breeze introduced us.

"Hey, y'all," I said hugging all of them.

I had not met any of my family on my father's side and I didn't feel any connection to any of them. Fighting hard to not blame them for just meeting, I smiled. I lived my entire life in Chicago and this was our first time talking to one another. Hell, I'd never seen them in passing. That did something to me, and I felt like an outsider.

"When did you get out of prison?" Nikki asked.

Nikki knowing I was locked up only heightened my irritation. I didn't even know these muthafuckas, but they knew my fuckin' business as if we've been connected since the sandbox. The shit didn't sit well with me, and I was no longer willing to fake the funk.

"How did you even know I was serving time? I don't know anything about you, but you know a lot about me."

"It's not even like that, Honey. We heard what happened to you and even tried to get you a better lawyer. Your mother wouldn't tell us anything to help us with the process. We've all been looking for your daddy but he's nowhere to be found. There has been no trace of him in damn near twenty years, per the adults in the family. We've always wanted to meet you, but it was Vickie who kept you away from our side of the family. That woman didn't want you around us at all. I'll be the first to apologize for not trying harder to get to know you."

The way Nikki explained things let me know that she was truly apologetic. There was nothing my cousins could do to develop a relationship with me because they weren't that much older. The fact that they were trying to get to know me now was what mattered the most at that point. I'd never had any family outside of Cheno and Breeze, and I was ready to let the other side in. Family is something I wished to have for years.

"I appreciate all y'all have done to get to know me. I won't hold what my mother did against y'all."

"Well, it's time to have some fun," Shon said with a smile.

"First, what's this I hear about Cheno being dead?" Cleve asked looking at Breeze. She glanced around to see who was in earshot and turned back to the cousins.

"I really don't want to talk about this right now, but Cheno is not dead. Let that stay right here," Breeze explained. "There are some niggas who tried to take him out and they didn't succeed. I put word out that he was dead so the muthafuckas responsible for shooting him can put down their guard."

"Who the fuck did that shit?"

"Come to my crib tomorrow and we can talk about it. There are too many ears around and there's no telling who may be listening. Until then, go get something to drink and enjoy the night."

"Yeah, I'll definitely be there. I can't believe you been dealing with this by yo'self, Breeze."

"That's the way my brother taught me to be. No disrespect against y'all. I had to make sure Cheno was safe. I don't know who else is trying to eliminate him."

"What you trying to say? You don't trust family?" Keyshae snapped.

"Not at all. We will talk about it tomorrow. This is not the place to go in depth about this shit. I'd advise you to lower yo' tone when talking to me, Keyshae'. You of all people knows how I get down."

Breeze walked away and flamed up before sitting down. I had to use the bathroom all of a sudden and excused myself from the group. Shon followed me down the stairs and I turned slowly.

"You going with me to the bathroom?" I asked.

"Um, yes. I don't allow anyone I'm with to wander around along. There have been too many females going missing from wandering off by themselves. So keep going because I'll be right there with you."

I couldn't do nothing but respect her having my back. The line to the bathroom was long as fuck and I didn't know how long I would be able to hold the urine that was threatening to come out of me. As the line started to move forward, someone bumped me into Shon with much force. Looking over my shoulder at the culprit, I came eye to eye with Letty and her sisters Shaveen and Shalonda.

"Bitch, watch where you going!" Letty hissed.

"I didn't move. You purposely walked into me. This ain't what you want, Letty. And I got yo' muthafuckin' bitch. When I fucked you up the last time you didn't have all the courage you have today. The shit will only be worse for you."

Shalonda took a step forward and I got into a boxer stance to handle her big back ass. She was the one that always jumped to help her shit talking sister when Letty talked too fuckin' much and couldn't back up what she said. They must've didn't realize I wasn't the same bitch they knew back in the day.

"Honey, we know for a fact you ain't on shit. You couldn't fight then and I doubt if you got your weight up now. I'm about to beat your ass and embarrass you for all to see."

Shalonda swung at my head and I dodged that shit like a pro boxer. Shalonda was all talk. I threw a two-piece combo and laid her ass out. I saw Letty approach from my right and when she was close enough, I started fucking her up. Letty was screaming for help but over the music, her cries went unheard. Grabbing her lil' ass around the neck I slammed her to the floor like a fuckin' wrestler. I was grabbed from behind by a couple of guys. As they pulled me away, I saw Shon in the middle of the floor working Shaveen's ass over before she was swept off her feet too.

"Nah, y'all gotta take that shit outside," The same bouncer that allowed us inside said. "Shon, you already know this is not the type of establishment for this type of shit."

"You know what, Fats, you right. Put they ass out and I'm right behind them." She snapped fighting to get out of his grasp.

By that time, someone had told Breeze what was going on. The whole crew were ready to rumble at that point. Letty and her sisters were still talking mad shit and I was ready to fuck them bitches up the right way. We were escorted out and guided off the property. Meaning we had to go across the street. Soon as we were let go, I kicked my heels off and went after Letty's bitch ass. She backed up and lost her footing and I was on her ass. I got hit from behind but that shit didn't faze me at all. I was zeroed in on the hoe I wanted to beat into a coma.

"Ain't no muthafuckin' jumping! Fuck that," Breeze hollered. "Y'all gon' stay right the fuck there and wait y'all turn."

I was beating Letty's ass while she was on the ground. She was kicking and flaring her arms around to get me off her. I did one better and snatched her by the hair then helping the bitch stand to her feet.

"Square up. I don't want you going around telling nobody I snaked yo' weak ass." Letty lunged at me and I hit her in her mouth without blinking. "Talk yo' shit now, bitch. All that scuffling ain't how I get down. I'm gon' beat yo' ass while you watch."

"Fuck you, Honey!"

Letty swung wildly and I knew she was discombobulated from the punched I'd thrown moments before. I chuckled because the shit just wasn't fair. Grabbing her by the front of

83

the little ass dress she wore, I punched her in the side of the head and didn't stop.

"Somebody get her off me!" Letty cried out.

Lowering her head to protect her face, I went underneath chin checkin' her ass with every punch I threw. I was fucking her up. Her nose started leaking and that shit brought a smile to my face. Putting the icing on the cake, I punched her hard as hell in the left eye and she fell flat on her back.

"Next time you come for me bitch, have your weight up. Don't bring that bullshit to me no mo'." I turned around searching for her bitch ass sisters and zoomed in on Shalonda. "Bring yo' big back ass on!"

"I'm just going to get my sister and we out of here." She said trying to walk around me.

Instead of letting her leave, I stole on her ass. She ducked her head and swung her arm trying to push me back. Her actions inside the club were quite different from what she displayed outside. I wasn't going to let her off that easy, the bitch had to stand on that bully shit. Hiking my dress up, I hit her ass with a combo causing her knees to buckle. Shalonda's head rock with ever punch I laded and I hoped to knock some sense into her ass.

The training I had in prison qualified my hands to be deadly weapons. Unfortunate for her, the shit wasn't on record. I could've killed that hoe if I wanted to, but I decided to take it light on her scary ass. Not too much though because I made sure to lump her ass up. Hitting her once more in the top of her head like a whack-o-mole, I finally let the bitch run off. I had one more sister to beat the fuck out of but she was saved by the bell.

Sirens could be heard in the distance and the last thing I needed was being back behind bars. I backed away from Shaveen and she hauled ass to the car her sisters had jumped into. Breeze was in the middle of the street and the sirens were getting closer.

"Honey, we got to get the fuck outta here! The laws' coming!" Breeze yelled.

Fats walked up to me and I was still skeptical about the newfound family members. "We will chop it up tomorrow at Breeze's. Just know, we will be here for you any way you need us to be."

I nodded and made my way to the parking lot. There was nothing I really wanted to say in response to what Fats said because why do they want to be there for me now? As I rushed to my car, the thoughts of how I was going to welcome them into my life plagued my mind. Soon as I opened the door to my Porsche, I heard Letty's voice in the distance.

"It ain't over, Honey!"

I laughed as I got in my whip pushing the start button. Breeze was sitting in her car with the window down. Lowering mine, I waited for her to say what was on her mind. Truthfully, I wanted to follow them hoes to beat their ass some more.

"The bitch still talking. We might as well let them get this shit off their chest tonight. I have more important shit to worry about than a bunch of bitches itching to get fucked up."

"Say less," I said putting the gear in drive. My cousin was on the same time I was on and I was with the shit.

Breeze backed out of the spot and I followed suit. Everybody else fell in line and it was on from there. Letty pulled out into traffic and Breeze had her black-on-black Benz on the radar. Never taking my eyes off what was going on in front of me, I drove with caution because anything was bound to happen. We'd been driving for a minute and I didn't know where we were headed. Then, my phone rang. Answering from the dash, it was a group call that Breeze started.

"Where the fuck we going?" Charlie asked.

"Just drive because I can see we're on a mission."

"You got that shit right, Spank." Breeze cut in. "Y'all strapped?"

"Hell yeah!"

"Always," I said without thought.

"Good. These hoes look like they're heading out west. If they're going where I think they're going, I need everybody who can without crashing to bust at everything on the block. We may as well start the war now!"

The anger in Breeze words were evident that she meant business. She was out to avenge Cheno and I was ready to stand ten toes down with her. Even though my conscious was telling me to put a stop to her plan, another side of me wanted the shit to go down. I knew the plan I'd conjured up wasn't going to work in my favor because Cheese was about to know somebody on Cheno's side clapped back.

"I thought we were only going to fight." Taz could be heard saying.

"If you scared, say that! I can pull over and let you out now. Uber the fuck home and wait for me to get there!"

"Breeze, Fredo said—"

"Fuck what he said! These muthafuckas tried to kill my brother! Now we're about to take a few of them out for what they did! Now, are you rollin' or not because I don't have all fuckin' night to negotiate with you, Taz."

The line went dead indicating Breeze ended the call. I reached into my purse and placed my Glock in my lap. We entered the expressway heading west. Taz must've agreed to the plan because Breeze never stopped to let her out. She was driving like a bat out of hell and I was right behind her switching lanes. Letty tried her best to shake Breeze but couldn't no matter how hard she tried. Letty exited on Congress Parkway and bent the corner on Homan. Breeze braked and slowed us down then the phone rang once again.

"They going on Trumbull. Honey, you and Charlie hit 15th and me and Spanky going up 16th. Light that muthafucka up then haul ass! Got it?" Breeze barked.

"Let's do it," Charlie said.

Turning my headlights off before turning down 15th, I could see Breeze creeping up the street from the 16th entrance of Trumbull. Letty was standing outside of her car talking to who I thought was Cheese. I put a bullet in the chamber and floored my truck. I had the passenger window down and pulled the trigger repeatedly. Bullets flew toward the building and bodies scattered like roaches. We were in and out of there within seconds leaving the scene the same way we came. Fast.

"Everybody good?" Breeze asked.

There were responses from everyone involved and that was good enough for me. The bullshit was in full effect and we were gonna have to watch our backs from that point on. But I was ready for whatever because what was done needed to happen.

Chapter 8

Cheese

Letty called telling me she was in an altercation with Honey at G-Spot. When she told me they were following them and didn't know what was going to happen, I automatically directed Letty to where I was. If Honey wanted to squabble, I was ready to open 15th and Trumbull up for them to handle business. That way I would have full control of how far the fight would go on.

"Nigga, we not about to get in the middle of this female shit." Tank roared. "Letty leading them bitches to our spot! Use yo' head, Cheese! You do know Cheno people looking for us, right?"

"Fuck that! They don't know shit about out here. These are females who's trying to throw hands." I laughed. "And don't nobody know who gunned that nigga Cheno down. He ain't here to tell. Calm yo' ass down."

Letty pulled up and jumped out of her car. I could see her sisters inside looking behind them. I met her halfway and she started going off like I was the one who fought her. Letty's lip was busted and she had a cut under her eye. Her jaw was swelling and the lace front she had installed a couple days ago was a mess. I could truly say, Honey did a number on my baby.

"That bitch is going to get hers. I guess they got scared and went about their business because they weren't following us when we turned off Homan. I'm telling you now, Cheese, I'm beating Honey's ass the next time I see her."

"Letty, I'm not gon' lie. When you first called, I was all for you going toe to toe with Honey. Now, the shit is over. Leave it at that. Y'all too grown for this type of play."

Letty looked at me through slitted eyes. "There you go protecting her ass again. You too passive when it comes to the bitch, Cheese. You. Don't. Know. Honey. Anymore! She's going to be your downfall. Watch."

Her jealousy was showing and Letty didn't realize how wrong her assumption was. I wasn't paying Honey any attention on the level Letty was speaking. Even though I'd thought about contacting her, I never acted on it. Mainly because Tank took it upon himself to put a hit out on Cheno. Soon as I was about to respond to Letty, movement caught my attention from the 16th street end of the block.

"Take cover!" I screamed pushing Letty to the ground.

Just as I thought, bullets flew in every direction and it sounded like a warzone and I was pissed. Whoever was busting on my spot had a lot of fuckin' ammo. Glass could be heard shattering around us and there was nothing I could do to return fire. The sound of tires peeling away was music to my ears. Without Letty's car protecting us, me and Letty could've for sure gotten hit. She was crying as I raised up off her.

"Letty, Shalonda was shot!" Shaveen called out as she got out of the car.

Rushing over to check on Letty's sister, I automatically took my shirt off and tied it around Shalonda's arm to stop the bleeding. Luck was on her side because her injuries could've been far worse than what it was. The passenger window was shot completely out. I didn't know what the other side looked like, but that would have to wait until later.

"I need you to get her to the hospital."

"Come with me. Tank can handle things here."

"That's not how shit works, Letty. I have to make sure everybody is straight. The block is hot and I need you far away from here. Plus, Shalonda needs to get checked out. Call me soon as you make it home. Do not come back over here," I said hugging Letty to my chest. "If the doctors at the hospital call the police, y'all don't know shit and didn't see shit. You hear me?" she nodded and backed out of my arms.

"I'll see you later. Shalonda, I'll check on you in a minute, sis."

"Cheno, I bet them bitches did this," Shaveen said from the backseat.

"I doubt it. This is the work of real shooters. There's no way a female did this type of damage. Trust me."

Letty smacked her lips and walked to the driver side of her car. She paused and I knew there was damage done to it.

"There's bullet holes in my shit, Cheese!"

"Get in the fuckin' car and take your sister to the hospital. I can't do nothing about that car right now. It will get taken care of tomorrow."

I watched Letty pull away from the curb and turned to see where Short was. Glancing around, it was chaotic on the block. Muthafuckas were checking on the homies that were down. I didn't think anybody was hit fatally, but I was wrong. Lord was propped with his back against the building and his head fell oddly to the side. That told me right away that he was gone.

"Fuck!" my head dropped to my chest as I walked slowly toward Lord. "Short, get over here!"

"Give me a minute, Sway is hit!" he yelled back.

Lord was dead and there was nothing I could do for him so I jogged over to where Short was. He was tending to a gunshot wound on Sway's legs. Seeing it wasn't serious, I took the time to tell them about Lord.

"Lord is dead. The Law will be through here so I hope everything is out of the way."

Short shook his head as he looked up at me. He opened his mouth to speak but Tank walked over while barking orders to the homies. When he got to me, anger was written on his face.

"I told yo' ass not to bring that shit over here, Cheese. Those bitches opened fire on us and we wasn't ready for the work they put in."

"You stupid as hell. I know for a fact Honey ain't no muthafuckin' shooter. This was done by the hands of niggas. If Honey followed Letty over here, she wouldn't have opened fire knowing I was out here."

Tank laughed. "You don't get it, do you, Cheese? We had her family killed, nigga. Honey is against you like everybody else on that nigga's team."

"You orchestrated that shit without my knowledge. I'm tied into this shit because you are my blood and I'll be a pussy ass nigga not to have your back. Whether you wrong or not, I'm gon' ride with you."

"I told you I wasn't waiting for you to come up with a plan, Cheese so I made the move. Waiting on you ain't no telling what would've happened!'

"Now look at the shit that just happened! We lost a muthafucka and many more are hurt including Letty's sister! Nigga, have a fuckin' heart right now. Niggas came busting and we wasn't ready for that shit!" I screamed in his face.

"If you wasn't in that bitch face you would've been ready."

"What's yo' excuse? Nothing was occupying yo' time when shit went left. Tell me why the fuck you weren't ready since you want to blame me!"

"Come on y'all, we gotta get out of here and get Sway to the doctor. I called and told him to meet me at the safe house."

I turned and walked away from Tank to help Short get Sway in his whip. Tank was a walking timebomb and shit was only going to get worse. I brought him into my operation so I could keep an eye on him and in turn, he was bringing more heat than I needed. With the shooting, I was being forced to shut down 15th street until further notice. Missing out on money was something I didn't want to do, but it needed to be done.

After I helped Sway in the whip, I took one last look at Lord. His mother was about to be crushed and all I could think to do was make sure she was able to bury her son. Of course, I was going to make sure she was straight financially, but it wasn't going to make her feel any better with Lord being gone.

I hopped in my vehicle and led the way to the safe house leaving Tank to handle the block. At some point, we were gonna have to sit down and lay out ground rules. Tank and his reckless actions were going to get many more people killed. I wasn't trying to be one of them.

As I drove up the street, red and blues were coming in the opposite direction. I turned right fast as I could because I wasn't trying to get pulled over once my vehicle was spotted. The pigs would automatically assume I had something to do with the shooting. They would be correct but a nigga like me would deny that shit 'til I was blue in the face. 15th Street was all me but I had other niggas running the shit. CPD had speculations of me being involved with no proof. It had been a minute since there was any heat on the block and I tried to keep it that way. Unfortunately, we were under fire and I had to figure out how to handle it.

Fifteen minutes later, I pulled into the driveway of the safe house in Maywood. Doc was waiting patiently on the porch smoking a cigarette. When I stepped out of the car, he plucked his butt into the bushes.

"Cheese, long time no see."

"Yeah, it's been a while, Doc. Help Short get Sway inside for me."

Jogging up the steps, I grabbed Doc's medical bag and entered the code to unlock the door. They carried Sway inside and took him to the back room, securing the place. I joined them putting Doc's bag within his reach. He cut Sway's pants leg then examined the wound. He looking inside his bag moving things around.

"That was a nasty hit. What happened?" Doc asked.

"Doc, I don't pay you to be in my business. He was shot. That's it, that's all. Is he going to be aight?" I retorted.

"There is no exit wound. Without x-ray, I have to use my better judgement and hope for the best," he said filling a syringe.

Giving Sway a shot in his shoulder, my nigga was out like a light within minutes. Doc then filled a second syringe and shot the medicine around the wound. He pulled a pair of gloves over his hands then started pressing on Sway's leg.

"Aha!" Doc exclaimed excitedly. "The bullet is still lodged in there. It most likely didn't hit a main artery because he isn't bleeding out. I can definitely fix him. He's going to be upset because what I have to do is going to leave an ugly scar."

"I'm quite sure Sway would rather have a scar versus losing his leg, or his life. Do what needs to be done, Doc," I said walking to the door after noticing him pull a scalpel from his bed. "I'll be in the other room. Come see me when you're done."

I may have been a strong nigga, but nothing in this world would allow me to watch Doc cut into Sway's leg. He was on his own with that mess. He had the experience; not me. Sitting down on the couch, I pulled out my phone and call Letty. The phone rang then went to voicemail. I took that as a sign of her being somewhere in the hospital without service.

Curiosity got the best of me and I took a chance of looking up Honey on social media. Her page was private and all I could see was the one photo she had as her profile picture. My dick bricked up from just the sight of her. Honey was no longer the young lady who used to ride me into submission back in the day. She grew into her body and filled that muthafucka out perfectly. Fuck milk doing a body good. Prison got her right. Her stomach was flatter than a board and the leggings she wore left nothing to my imagination. Her camel toe looked like it was reaching out for a nigga.

The thoughts going through my mind had me in a chokehold. I couldn't believe how I was contemplating a plan to get back with Honey. With the beef she and Letty had going on, that should've been the last thing for me to think about. Since seeing Honey at the club, I've had many regrets of not being there for her. Correcting my wrongs with her was something I really wanted to do but there was a slim to none chance of that happening because of what occurred with Cheno. My phone vibrated in my hand and Letty's face appeared on the screen.

"Hey, how's Shalonda?" I asked soon as I answered.

"She had to get eight stitches. They took x-rays and gave her a tetanus shot. Other than that, the bullet went in one side and came out the other. The doctor said it was a clean shot and Shalonda was lucky. I'm on my way to drop Shaveen off now."

"Okay cool. Call if you need me. Go straight home, Letty."

"I am. What time will you be there?" she asked.

"Right now, I don't know. I'll call when I'm on the way though."

"Yeah, okay." She sassed and hung up.

Letty had an attitude for whatever reason but I didn't have the energy to call back arguing with her. She knew how serious the situation was but wanted to pull that jealous shit. Her insecurities about Honey were going to be the cause of her heartbreak. One thing a female needed to learn was not push a nigga into the arms of another bitch with accusations. If there wasn't proof of wrong doing, leave that shit alone. That alone led me back to social media and right into Honey's inbox.

Makin' Cheddar Hawkins

What's up, Honey? I know I'm the last nigga you want to hear from. We started off on the wrong foot , so I wanted to apologize for how I handled you at the club. On some real shit, you look good as fuck! LOL Seriously, Honey, I miss you. I already know what you gon' say. I can explain why you haven't heard from me. Can you just hear me out?

It was late and Honey wasn't online. However, before I could exit out of the app, the green light came on indicating she had logged in. Waiting patiently for her to read the message I left for her, the bubbles appeared then disappeared several times. I watched the screen for what seemed like forever. I could feel in my soul that she was cussing me out badly and I deserved every bit of what she was about to dish out. All I could do was wait. She finally sent the message and damn, she had a lot to get off her chest.

Honey Love

LaDarrius, you have some nerve contacting me! Nigga, I took a charge for your muthafuckin ass and I served a decade in the prison system just for you to leave me in there to rot by myself. What happened to "I'm gon' hold you down"? That lasted what, twelve months? I want you to know that was low down for somebody who claimed they loved me. If that's what you call love, you can have that shit. The same way you lost contact with me for the past nine years, keep the same energy now that I'm back on the street. The bullshit you pulled at the club made you look like a goofy. I couldn't believe you acted out the way you did while your bitch was present.

Since I'm on the subject, you could've fucked around with anybody, but you chose my bum ass ex best friend. The one that couldn't stand you and you hated her just as much. I know why now, but that don't even matter to me. I whooped her ass because she broke the fuckin' code! It didn't have nothing to do with you. Don't get it twisted. I want you to keep Letty away from me, LaDarrius. I've beaten her ass twice. The third time would be the last.

Out of everything Honey said, I focused on the fact that she didn't mention Cheno's death. Taking that as a sign of them not knowing or implementing him and his crew as being behind the shooting. I breathed a sigh of relieve and my heart started beating at a normal rate as I continued to read.

I don't want to be the reason you have to bury your bitch and explain to her family that your ex was the one to put her in the dirt. Far as hearing your lame excuse about why I haven't heard from you, don't bother. You showed me how you move and yeah, it means nothing to me. I'm not the same little girl that got knocked behind bullshit, LaDarrius. I learned a lot in prison and the most important lesson was never depend on somebody that isn't true to their word. It takes one time for a muthafucka to shit on me and you already had your turn.

I sat looking at my phone in shock because Honey wasn't the same girl she was when she was with me. Prison hardened her and I didn't know how I was going to break the mold for forgiveness. There was so much venom in her words, and the way she didn't back down from telling me how she felt, I knew Honey was all woman. I didn't sense an ounce of hurt. Honey was pissed the fuck off and I caused that shit. There was no telling what she had endured behind the walls of that prison and I didn't have the right to ask. In a way, I abused her too because I left her hanging.

Makin' Chedda Hawkins

Honey, I want you to know that I was not fuckin' around with Letty before you went to prison. I wouldn't have ever disrespected you like that. Getting in a relationship wasn't supposed to happen but it did. She filled the void of you not being there with me. I'm sorry. Letty told me about the altercation y'all had tonight. I already told her that both of y'all are too old for this back-and-forth shit. Now, I'm going to tell you, leave it alone. Y'all fought and it's over.

I really want us to get to know one another again, Honey. I wasn't lying when I said I miss you. Since I saw you at the club, you're all I think about. Let me take you out. If everything goes in our favor, maybe we can rekindle what we had on some grown up shit this time.

It was a slim chance to none that Honey would take my apology with a grain of salt. She was going to let me know how much she hated me and demand I never contacted her again. I was prepared to take that shit to the chin. As bad as I wanted Honey in my life again, I wasn't going to hold my breath to wait for her response. Shid, I was contemplating leaving Letty alone for her. Even though I put on the persona to Letty that I wasn't thinking about Honey, that was a baldfaced lie. The bubbles reappeared and my erection tightened in my pants. Her lil young ass had a gushy tunnel as an eighteen-year-old. I could only imagine what it felt like now that she was older and a born-again virgin. The thought alone had me squeezing my shit to calm him down.

Honey Love

I don't believe you were crazy enough to fuck my best friend under my nose. What I can't believe is that you didn't waste any time getting with her! If you needed comfort, you should've bought a throw blanket and some socks, nigga! You want to prove you miss me, and you want forgiveness...leave the bitch. That's the only way I would give you an inkling of my time. I will not be the bitch who went from the main to the side chick. When you release the hoe from your nut sack, holla at me. Until then, don't contact me anymore. Be safe out there, Cheese.

I read the message several times because something wasn't right about the words Honey used. I didn't think too hard on it because I had one job. To get Letty out of my life so I could have Honey back where she belonged. By my side.

***

Walking into my home at damn near six in the morning, a nigga was beyond tired. Sway was going to be alright but he had to rest and heal in order to get better. I paid Doc and thanked him for his services and left Short to look after him while I went home to get some sleep. He also informed the workers to take the day off with pay until I got back with them. Soon as I took my shoes off at the door, Letty was standing at the top of the stairs with a scowl on her face.

"You let the sun beat you in this house and we said that shit was never supposed to happen. Where you been, Cheese?"

"Letty, don't start with that shit. You were in the midst of the bullshit that went on earlier. Yo' sister got hit and she's lucky it was just a shot to the arm. Two of my men were shot and one didn't make it. Why are you asking stupid as questions when you know I had to handle shit on my end? That was my spot and I'm the boss that has to make sure everything is straight."

"If that's what you were doing, come here and let me smell yo' dick. If you don't smell like sweat, I'm punching you in yo' shit!"

I walked slowly toward the stairs with a slick smirk on my face. Letty was in for a rude awakening because she was on bullshit and I was ready to make her pay for accusing me. We just had a conversation about her attitude and she still wanted to push me. When I was standing in front of her, Letty wasted no time unbuckling my belt and my pants. She looked up at me before kneeling on her knees. She was eye to eye with my wood and I didn't stop her from completing her inspection. Reaching into my underwear, she pulled my member out like it was a boa constrictor. Letty inhaled the aroma smacking her lips. She rose up and I pushed her ass back into position.

"Nah, you may as well finish the job you started. Ain't no way you gon' brick my shit up and leave it in that condition. Suck that muthafucka, Letty."

"I'm not about to suck your dick and it smell salty as hell! You got me fucked up, Cheese," Letty said loudly rise up to stand. Once again, I pushed her back to her knees.

"I didn't ask you to suck my shit. I'm telling you to drain this nut out. Get ya jaws ready because I need to bust."

Shaking my dick in her face, Letty opened her mouth to protest and I stuck that muthafucka down her throat. She tried to pull back and I gripped the back of her head. I move my hips and paused.

"If your teeth scrape my shit or you even think about biting me, we gon' have a problem. You stalling and my nuts are full. Let's go."

Letty started sucking my dick like Superhead. She had never topped me off on the level she was doing at that moment. My toes dug deep in the carpet and I was struggling to keep my balance. Letty was sucking my soul through my muscle and the shit had me weaker than a muthafucka. I wanted to stop her for a minute but her mouth felt too good to put a halt to her actions.

"Fuck, Letty. Shit." I hissed. "From this point on, this is how you suck my dick!"

I let all my babies glide down her throat causing my eyes to roll in the back of my head. Letty swallowed every drop, and my erection was still harder than a steel pipe. There was no way she got all the semen out of my sack. I stepped back and grabbed the handrail so I wouldn't fall. Letty had a scowl on her face as if she wanted to kill me. She got up and turned her back to head into the bedroom. I reached out and grasped her arm and she snatched away. Allowing her to think I would let her walk away; I followed behind her.

I pulled my pants off and tossed them in the middle of the hall. Letty was about to enter the bathroom when I circled my arm around her waist. She wiggled to get out of my grasp, and I cupped her coochie with the palm of my hand.

"Ain't no way I'm about to fuck you, Cheese. Get off me," she snarled. "Treating me like a hoe on the street and expect me to throw this ass in a circle is pure blasphemy."

Instead of responding to her, I slipped my middle finger inside her box and caressed her slippery folds. Letty was saying one thing, but my little girlfriend with the thick lips was screaming another. She threw her head back into my chest and moaned loudly. Yeah, there was no way Letty could deny me of my pussy.

"Cum for me, baby."

"No, Cheese. I'm mad at you," she whined.

Moving my finger in and out of her center, I inserted another finger, then wrapped my other hand around her throat. I lowered my head so my mouth was against her ear.

"I call the shots around here, you know that. All you have to do is comply to my demands. Now, do you want to do this your way, or the hard way? Don't worry about it. I got this."

I lifted her off her feet and hoisted her against the wall. Letty knew what was about to happen and the anger in her eyes turned to lust instantly. Her clean shaved yoni was exposed in my face and my mouth watered. Using the weight of my chest to hold her up, I placed her legs on my shoulders and dove right into her snatch. Letty cupped the back of my head in the same manner I did hers moments before.

"Oooooouuu shit! Eat your pussy, baby," she purred, grinding her hips.

My face was drenched in her essence, and it coated my tongue perfectly. The sweetness of her juices had me forgetting I was supposed to be coming up with a plan to get Letty out of my life. There was no way possible I could leave her so another nigga could stake claim to the goods.

"I'm cummin'! Oh shit, Cheese. Suck it, baby. Suck it!"

Doing as I was told, Letty let all her juices flow and at that moment I knew exactly what Gerald LeVert meant when he made that song. I know Honey wanted me all to herself, but I would have to play my cards right to keep both women in my life for the long haul. Giving Letty's lower lips a few kisses, I placed her on the floor then pecked her on the lips. She wanted this dick, but a nigga was too tired for that. Licking the attitude out of her was my main objective and I accomplished that easily.

"There's nobody but you, Letty. The quicker you learn that, the better. It's me and you 'til the end of time."

I left her standing there and went into the bathroom to start the shower. The lies rolled off my tongue with no problem. Letty wasn't going anywhere, but I damn sure was going to get a taste of Honey soon enough.

Chapter 9

Breeze

The night before was crazy. I never wanted to pull Honey into any street shit but there was no way I could miss the opportunity to light up 15th Street. Our crew handled that shit with ease, and nobody chumped up. We all went our separate ways then checked in once everybody was safely home. I made sure to let it be known that we didn't know shit. Which didn't need to be explained but I put it out there. I rolled over and Taz was stretched out on the bed like a damn octopus with her cat exposed. Soon as I got into the sniper position, the damn doorbell sounded. I sighed heavily, crawled toward the nightstand and grabbed my phone. I opened the app for the ring camera and my cousins were on the porch.

"Man, what the fuck y'all doing here so early?" I asked through the app.

"Breeze, open the door." Cleve said putting his face close to the camera.

Covering Taz's body with the sheet, I pulled on a pair of shorts and tank before slipping my feet in my slides. Going into the bathroom, I gargled with mouthwash to hold me over until I could brush properly. I left the room, closing the door then went downstairs to let the three amigos inside. Nikki and Shon entered behind Cleve while I locked up.

"Why didn't you cook?" Shon asked.

"I didn't know I had to. When I said come to my crib, I didn't mean bright and early," I said gesturing for them to go into the living room.

"Under the circumstances, this shit couldn't wait. What happened when y'all left the club last night? I was looking for y'all after they put y'all out."

"Cleve, Honey beat the fuck out of them bitches by her lonesome. That's what happened. You saw for yourself that they were trying to jump her. What Letty and her sister's didn't expect was Honey to take them all on one on one. We were deep, but Honey needed to whoop them hoes the way she did." I laughed walking over to the crystal bowl on the coffee table.

"I know that part, Breeze. You must not have seen the news this morning."

"Nah, I just woke up when you disturbed my peace. What happened that I should know about?" I asked filling a Wood with weed.

"There was a shooting on 15th Street. Two people were shot, one of them died. From what I know, that is Cheese territory, and the females y'all were fighting are associated with him. Did you have anything to do with that?"

Licking the blunt then closing it tightly, I picked up a lighter and flamed up. After taking a couple puffs, I sat back, staring my big cousin in the eye. Cleve waited patiently for me to speak, and I didn't want to leave him in suspense too long.

"That had everything to do with me and I'll tell you why," I said passing the blunt to Shon and started rolling another. "If you think I shot up that block over some bitch shit, you wrong. It's deeper than that. There's always a method to my madness, Cleve. You know that."

"Okay, tell me what the fuck I need to know."

"The niggas out west, on 15th Street is the reason my brother is laid up in a coma. It's good to know one of them is living their best life in hell, but there's many more to follow." I paused. "A nigga named Tank ran up in Cheno spot on the Nine and hit him for all he had in that muthafucka. The robbery was clean as fuck so, we know for a fact it was an inside job. Cheno found out who was behind the shit and that's how Tank was identified. Then, we learned Tank was Cheese's cousin."

"Cheese that run the entire west side?"

"Yeah, him. Anyway, Cheno and some of the lil niggas went and shot up Tank's mama's crib. Things were quiet for a couple weeks before Cheese or his cousin used a bitch to lure Cheno out to be killed. Except, they didn't kill him. I put that information in the street to protect him, so they won't go looking to finish the job."

"So, Cheno is alive?" Nikki asked.

"Didn't you hear me say he was in a coma last night? That's not dead. Cheno gon' bounce back. We just have to wait until he's ready to open his eyes. The nigga just resting right now."

"Damn. Why didn't you call me, Breeze? I know Cheno got a small army of niggas, but nothing compared to what Cheese has. There's no way y'all can go up against him without help. I'm down to come out of retirement to handle business."

"I appreciate that, Cleve. Turning down help isn't an option. You're right. We do need more shooters. Cheno's boy Quell has some of his hittas coming up from Atlanta, then I got the girls on board. Plus the crew that will ride for Cheno without question."

"Can you trust them muthafuckas though? Didn't you say the robbery was an inside job?" I nodded as I blew smoke from my mouth. "Then they damn sure can't be trusted."

"Nah, the only person that has been moving funny is Free. He hasn't been back around since the trap was hit. Nobody can get in touch with him or nothing. I know deep down he's the one we need to find and it's off with his muthafuckin' head right along with them westside niggas."

My phone buzzed in my pocket, and I pulled it out. Seeing Dawson's name on the screen made me chuckle. I declined the call and placed the device on the table. I hadn't heard from his deadbeat ass in nine years and now he was on my line. He could miss me with that bullshit. When my phone rang a second time, I automatically looked at my cousins with a sour taste in my mouth.

"Which one of y'all got this nigga Dawson calling me?"

Nikki looked down at her hands. "He came to my mama's house because he heard about Cheno getting killed. One of his people in the hood told him about it. He jumped down my throat asking why he wasn't called. I didn't have the answers he was looking for at the time, so I gave him your number. I'm sorry, Breeze."

"There's nothing for you to be sorry about. It's just ironic that he had to get my number from you when I have his number saved in my phone. Your uncle ain't shit and I believe he's on utter bullshit and that's why he's calling. Dawson don't give a fuck about me nor Cheno." In the midst of my rant, the muthafucka called again.

"Why are you blowing up my line?" I roared into the phone.

"Is that the way you speak to your father?"

"I wouldn't know because I don't have a father. The nigga walked out on my mother, never did shit for me, and ran like a racehorse once he found out I was a lesbian. Haven't seen his ass since." I smirked as I puffed my blunt.

"You still disrespectful as fuck I see." Dawson sneered. "I told yo' mama…"

"That's what you not gon' do. Leave my mama out of your shit because she ain't here to defend herself. I got her covered though. As far as me being disrespectful, is that what you call it? I would say there was a lot of truth in what I said. If it pissed you off, hit dogs holla." I laughed. "Come on, Dawson, what do you really want?"

"What happened to my son, Brianna?"

"That's the name you wanted for me. It never made the cut, Dawson. My name is Breeze. As far as your son goes, which one are you talking about? Dawson Jr or Dyshon?"

"Ricky! Cheno! My oldest son that I was told was killed! You didn't even call to tell me about the shit! I'm his fuckin' father!"

I laughed uncontrollably as I coughed like I was dying from the weed smoke. This negro was out of his mind, and he didn't realize I had his attitude down to a tee. Yeah, I was giving him unnecessary hell, but he deserved it, and I was getting a kick out of antagonizing his bum ass.

"This is not a joking matter, Breeze. I can still whoop your ass you know."

"And you would get shot between your fuckin' eyes." Ceasing all laughter. "I'm not a little girl anymore, Dawson. In fact, I don't even identify as one." The look on my cousin's faces made me start laughing all over again. The look of bewilderment was on full display. "Why are you all of a sudden claiming us as your kids? I mean, I'm trying to understand this shit like I'm a toddler. You haven't been around in forever. Cheno was the man of our house since he was a teenager. Why now, Dawson?"

I knew if I pushed him far enough, he would come out with the reason he popped back on the scene. The story he came up with about hearing Cheno died wasn't believable enough for me. If he truly gave a fuck, he would've been around long before tragedy struck. Hell, he didn't even send a note by Harry Potter's owl when my mama died. But he's calling about Cheno. Something fishy was in the water and I was going to find out what was causing the stench.

"I've always claimed y'all. You're making it seem like I favored my other kids more than you and Cheno."

"You did," I said with a chuckle. "Tell me the nature of this call, Dawson. I got shit to do and being on this phone humiliating you ain't one of them."

"Okay. I need Cheno's death certificate and you are the only person who can get it for me."

Hearing Dawson reveal his reason for reaching out to me made my blood pressure rise to compacity. I balled my fist tightly in my lap and wished like hell he was standing in front of me because I would've killed him. This muthafucka had his nerve coming to me on some come up type shit. Then, using my brother to do it.

"You mean to tell me you got a muthafuckin' insurance policy on my brother! Why would I give you a death certificate so you can collect a check and you ain't did shit for him? You are a poor excuse for a father! I bet yo' grimy ass reaped the benefits when my mama died too! I wouldn't put it past you if you were just paying for policies waiting for all of us to croak. Nigga, you ain't getting shit! Figure it out on your own. Fuck you, bitch!"

I ended the call and broke down. Usually, I wouldn't get emotional in front of anyone, but that shit wasn't so easy as of late. Shon and Nikki got up to console me, but I shook my head and held my hand up. I rose from the chair I was sitting in and left out the patio doors. I rested my arm on the brick exterior of my home and cried like a baby. Dawson had hurt me for the last time. All I've ever wanted since he left was for him to be a father to me. I shouldn't have had to beg and plead with him to accept me for who I was. The shit was a battle I wasn't going to fight.

"Mama, I need you," I wept. "I can't continue to be strong without you and Cheno. Why did you leave me out here alone?"

My soul quaked and I couldn't catch my breath. The more I tried to get control of myself, the more I cried. A pair of arms wrapped around my body. Taz's scent was the calm I didn't know I needed.

"It's gon' be alright, bae. Don't let your daddy get under your skin. I'm here for all your wants and needs. I promise."

"I appreciate that but please don't ever refer to that man as my daddy. I don't have one of those." I huffed. "Look, I'm good and thanks for coming out to check on me. Can you order something to eat? I have to run out and take care of some business in a little while."

"I'll cook something really quick. Anything in particular that you want?"

"Whatever you cook is fine. I appreciate you."

"I know you do," Taz said kissing me deeply.

"Tell my cousins to come out here for a minute. Roll me a fatty and bring it out before you go in the kitchen."

"I got you."

The entire conversation with Dawson took me out of character and I needed to shake that shit off. I wasn't going to allow it to take me down a dark hole because I was too damn strong to fold. What I did understand in it all was I was still human and had feelings. I just didn't need to get caught up in the rapture at that moment. Taz came back in no time and my cousins sat down on the patio furniture waiting for me to speak. Lighting the blunt until the cherry popped, I coughed.

"Breeze, you smoke too much." Nikki had the nerve to say. "You may be addicted to that shit."

"No disrespect to you but the last time I checked, weed is a muthafuckin' herb, not a drug. Maybe if you smoked some of this green it could've heightened your senses a little better. Then you would've known not to give your muthafuckin' uncle my number."

"I had nothing to do with how he came at you. That's your daddy and I figured it would be alright to give him your contact."

"Well, you figured wrong! That muthafucka haven't given a fuck about me and Cheno since we were shorties. You know that. He comes over to your mama house with his other kids and the bitch he left my mama for. How many times have you seen us with them as one big happy ass family? Never!" I replied, taking another pull. "Dawson's objective is to cash in on an insurance policy for a nigga that's still breathing. And that's why I want to talk to the three of y'all."

"I know Uncle Dawson didn't say no shit like that," Cleve spoke up.

"Like hell if he didn't. The nigga ain't shit. I want y'all to keep the narrative of Cheno being dead going. Dawson dirty ass may beat the streets to find somebody to kill my brother off if he knew otherwise. Cheno ain't safe being laid up in that hospital defenseless. His own fuckin' sperm donor is against him in the worse way."

"What about my mama?"

"What about her, Nikki?" I frowned.

"You know how much she loves Cheno. Her heart is hurting thinking he's gone. I have to tell her the truth."

Shaking my head, I pulled deeply on the blunt in my hand. Nikki must've had too much wax in her ears because I'd just told her not to tell anybody anything other than Cheno was dead. That included her mama. I loved my Aunt Roberta but she talked too fuckin' much for my liking. Plus, she would tell Dawson the truth even if it wasn't intentional.

"You're not going to tell her shit! I said, keep the shit between us. This is not me trying to hide shit out of spite, I'm protecting *my* bloodline. I'm telling you now, if something happens to him because you ran yo' muthafuckin' mouth, I'm beating yo' ass! And that's on my mama!"

"Breeze, we don't have to go there. I'll make sure word don't get out," Shon said. "I understand where you coming from with this. Dawson is dead wrong and when I see him, I'm gon' tell him a thang or two."

"I got that covered, sis," Cleve said turning to Nikki. "I want you to keep this from mama. It's too big of a risk to tell the truth now."

"I've never lied to her before, and she's been crying since I told her Cheno was dead."

"And she will be happier than a nigga on the low who came out of the closet when Cheno goes over to see her. Just remember what I said. Another thing, Kayshae had her panties in a bunch at the club. Make sure she doesn't say shit either. She's not exempt from getting socked. I have to get myself together so I can take care of some shit. Plus, I need to go see my brother. I'll keep y'all posted though."

"What hospital is he in? I want to go visit," Cleve said.

"Not gon' happen," I said walking back into the house.

"Breeze…"

"Cleve, I'll call you later. I've given y'all all the information I'm willing to reveal. Hell, Nikki is struggling to keep her mouth shut about him being alive. That's a hazard in itself. Go home, Roger."

I laughed walking up the stairs, leaving my cousins to see their way out. Taz would make sure to lock up. Entering the bedroom, I went right to my closet. It was the second week of August and hotter than a muthafucka too. I pulled a pair of black cargo shorts off the hanger and got a white wife beater from the drawer, lying everything on the bed. My mind was racing, and I couldn't concentrate on one task. Deciding to call Miss Pearl, I went into the bathroom and sat on the toilet.

"It took you long enough to call me, Breeze," Miss Pearl said without saying hello. "I don't want to discuss nothing over this phone. You better be at my house within the hour."

I opened my mouth to respond and the old muthafucka hung up on me. Miss Pearl better be glad I had respect for her, or I would've called back cussing her ass out. I started the water in the shower and stepped right in. One thing I knew was Miss Pearl didn't play. When she said be there, your ass better be walking up the steps five minutes before. I washed thoroughly and got out then brushed my teeth. After oiling my body, I walked back into the bedroom naked as the day I was born. It took no time for me to get dressed and slid my feet into a fresh pair of all-white Nikes.

Gathering my keys, wallet, phone, I snapped my watch on my wrist before spraying a little bit of Sauvage on my clothes. When I walked into the hall, the aroma of whatever Taz was cooking filled my nostrils. Heading straight for the kitchen, she was plating what looked like a patty melt with home fries. I sat at the table and Taz placed the food in front of me.

"Thanks, babe. Did you put mushrooms in it?"

"No, I didn't know you liked them," she said shrugging her shoulder.

"It's cool. I'm about to smash this shit anyway." Taking a bite, I moaned. "This hitting."

"Yeah, I know how to work my way around a kitchen. You know that. Anyway, what do you have to do today?"

"I'm going to find out some shit about what's being said on the street. Then, I'm going to head to the hospital to see Cheno. You staying here, or you want me to drop you off at the crib?" I asked biting into the sandwich that was too good to put down.

"I'll stay here, and you can drop me off when you get back. I have to be at the shop early to open up with Charlie."

"Fuck! I got an appointment at nine in the morning. Shit, I have two custom jobs to handle," I said looking at the time on my watch. "I gotta get out of here."

Standing to my feet, I grabbed the plate and Taz took it for me. I gave her a deep kiss while palming her ass. Our first go 'round with this relationship didn't work, but I was determined to do what was right and settle down. Taz was a good woman. I wasn't ready to give my all to just one before. With the shit I was experiencing in real time with Cheno and the other bullshit, life was definitely short and wasn't promised to anyone. I got lost in my thoughts but never missed a beat showering my girl with a little bit of affection.

"I'll be back soon as I can, big booty."

The smile Taz displayed let me know I was doing something right in our courtship. I left the house feeling better than earlier and was ready to feel the wrath of whatever Miss Pearl had planned for me. I knew I should've called or went by to tell her what happened to Cheno, but I didn't want to put that type of hurt on her until I knew Cheno was going to be alright. Miss Pearl was far from dumb. She knew shit that was going on the minute it happened and if somebody asked how, I wouldn't be able to tell them. It was like she had a satellite system set up around the city and she watched everything from the comfort of her home.

"To Be Honest" by Young Dolph was the song that came on when I connected my phone to the Bluetooth. Backing out of the driveway, I stepped on the brake to take in my home and smiled. Cheno really had me living well. Our lives were nothing like it was when we were living in the hood with our mother. Times were hard when Dawson decided to leave after saying he was going to the store to buy a case of Pepsi and a pack of cigarettes. Every time I thought about that story after Cheno told me about it, I laughed. That was a pussy ass move on his part. Why not just say you didn't want to be there anymore? I continued backing out of the driveway and headed to Miss Pearl's, still thinking about all we'd been through.

Regardless, when my mama wanted to relocate to Georgia, it was Cheno that made sure we moved into a home that he put in both his and my mama's name. My brother was the one that made sure there was food in the refrigerator, and clothes on my back. Mama and I didn't want for nothing because Cheno made sure of it. He was the man of the house, and I didn't have a choice but to respect him as if he was my daddy. The day my mama called Cheno over to talk, I would always remember what she said to us.

"Both of you know I love y'all to death, right?"

Both me and Cheno nodded, but my brother started fidgeting nervously. Me, I just sat stoically waiting to hear what she was about to lay on us. We had known for a few years that she was sick but was hoping for a miracle. I hadn't prepared myself for what I had learned about my mother that day.

"I went to the doctor earlier and they told me the cancer has spread. You all know I have never kept anything from you, and I won't start now. There is nothing more they can do for me. The chemo nor radiation will stop the growth."

My mother sat before us as if she was telling us a story about her childhood. She didn't look worried that the doctors basically told her she was going to die from the illness she had been fighting with all her might. My eyes stung from the tears which were threatening to fall, but I refused to allow them to drop. Being strong for her was my main objective.

"How long do you have?" Cheno asked solemnly.

"Six months." She chuckled. *"I know it's not funny but there's no need to cry about something I can't change. The doctors have done everything they can for me."*

"No, we can get a second opinion. It must be something else another doctor can do."

"Cheno, we already had a second, third, and fourth opinion. This is the last stage, and you have to live with the outcome." She rocked back and forth slowly while looking down at her feet. *"I've prepared for this moment and have everything planned so neither of you will have to. All of the paperwork is in the safe on the top shelf of my closet in the bedroom. The only thing I need y'all to do is get me the help I need if I'm still breathing but unresponsive."*

"I'm not ready for this, ma. We should still try to see if another doctor can help." Cheno expressed his concern.

"I'm done trying, Cheno. My body can't take any more of this. Whenever God decides to call me home, I'll be ready. We all have a time and date to leave this earth. We just don't know which day it will be. I wanted to prepare both of you for what lies ahead for me. My job is done here. It's time for you to step up more than you already have, son."

"This don't have to be the end! You are going to fight. Giving up is not the answer." Cheno cried. "I'm going to do my part and schedule an appointment with another oncologist first thing in the morning. Okay?"

"Okay, but it's not going to do any good. Cheno, I want you to take care of your sister. In order for you to do that, you have to leave the life you're living behind. Get out of the streets, baby. Breeze is going to need you."

"That's already understood. We are concentrating on you for the time being. Breeze is going to be okay."

Cheno found another doctor and the results were the same. There was nothing else to be done to cure my mother of the cancer that was eating away at her body. Every day was spent doing fun things and making memories. It was different at that moment because no one knew when the last day would be. The laughs filled us with so much life. Four months later, a week after we came back from a Jamaican cruise, my mother lost her battle.

Shaking my head to focus back on driving, I wiped my face because once again I was crying and I hated that. Anger replaced the sadness I felt because instead of Cheno being by my side, he was still resting in the hospital. It wasn't that I needed my brother as my protector, I wanted him there. My mother didn't think I could take care of myself, but after being out in the world alone, I didn't have a choice. Looking down at the time on the dash, it was ten minutes until I was supposed to pull up on Miss Pearl and I wasn't going to disappoint her because I was there.

"I was gearing up to strip a strap off that tree over there if you would've shown up late. Get your behind in this house."

Raising my windows, I got out and hit the key fob to lock the doors. Miss Pearl stood on the porch smoking a cigarette. She knew how much I hated to see her smoke those things. It was like pulling teeth to get her to quit.

"Put that cigarette out, Granny. You know they're not good for you."

"Keeping what you thought was secrets ain't good for you either! I guess we're both doing shit we're not supposed to be doing, huh?"

Pearl had a slick ass tongue and if you weren't careful, she could really hurt your feelings with just words. What she said didn't faze me because I learned to wear my armored skin when around her. I rolled my eyes as I passed her to enter the house. She popped me playfully in the back of my head.

"Roll 'em again and I will knock 'em right on the floor. Now tell me your version of what happened to Cheno, Breeze," Pearl said closing and locking the door.

As I explained everything I knew and had found out, she sat listening quietly. When she reached for the pack of Newports, I smacked her hand away causing her to scowl at me. Continuing, I gave Pearl an update on Cheno's condition and left out the shooting me and the girls did on 15th, nor did I tell her about Sia. She turned her body, so she was facing me.

"So, have you tracked down the little bitch that was messaging Cheno?"

"No, I tried calling the number and it's no longer in service. I got an address on her but I have yet to go check it out. It's kind of hot right now. In due time, I'm going pay her a visit."

"Did that pretty lil thang you used to deal with give you the information before you killed her?" I was shocked she even knew anything about that, and I started sweating around my collar because if Pearl knew, who else could've known.

"Don't be surprised. I have eyes everywhere. I even know who's responsible for the death of that boy out west on 15th. Nice job by the way." She smiled holding her hand up for a high five. "Okay, enough with the celebration. We are far from living life as we know it. Cheese and his crew are not going to take this lying down. They will come after anyone affiliated with Cheno. One doesn't have to be smart to know where the retaliation stemmed from. What I do know is, Cheno's crew isn't large enough to take on Cheese. While waiting for you to contact me, I did a little recruiting of my own. In fact, I had the ball rolling the moment I heard Cheno was shot."

Pearl rose from the couch and shuffled toward her bedroom. When she returned with a cigarette dangling from the corner of her mouth, all I could do was shake my head. Saying something about her habit was useless and I decided to just mind my damn business.

"Don't say shit, Breeze because you smoke mo' weed than Cheech and Chong put together. Your habit ain't no better than mine," she said hiking her moo-moo up before sitting down. "Anyway, my God granddaughter's husband called about some females fighting in his club. He sent over video for me to look at to see if I could identify the culprits. When I saw you and Honey, I had to tell him about Cheno. He wants to help and is working on finding that bitch Larisa as we speak. I'm waiting for him to get back with me. When I get more information, I'll make sure I reach out to you. Don't go to that address until I can verify it's legit." She took a puff from her cigarette and blew it to the left of her, away from me.

"In the meantime, baby, I need you to keep your cool. The time will come for you to get revenge. Just watch your back out there. I'm not telling you to run from no muthafucka. Handle your business if bullshit comes your way. But don't go looking for shit!" Pearl hissed. "What you did on 15th Street wasn't wrong. It wasn't the right time to take action. Honey should've whooped that hoe senseless and left it at that."

"I didn't start shit!" Pearl glared at me through slit eyes. "I'm sorry. I didn't start nothing. When I realized where Letty was headed, I reacted."

"Listen to me. You have to learn how to control yourself because every action doesn't need a reaction. I know you love Cheno and I do too, but we have to think rationally right now." Pearl studied my demeanor and believe me, I was listening. It was going to be hard for me to take heed to what she said.

"I went to the hospital and sat with Cheno for a while last night. I put that boy Mike out and prayed with my baby. As I held his hand, he squeezed mine a little bit. It will be a matter of time before he opens his eyes. You gotta have faith because I sure do."

Hearing that Cheno responded to her put a smile on my face. "You just made my day, Granny! I'm going up there soon as I leave here."

"That's what I like to see. Your beautiful smile and those damn dimples. Looking like your no-good ass daddy."

The smile fell from my face instantly. I hated when folks said I looked like Dawson's deadbeat ass. In my opinion, I looked like a replica of my mama. The only thing I inherited from that man was my height, and the dimples. That's it.

"Speaking of Dawson, he called me today because he heard Cheno was dead. Do you know he had the nerve to ask for the death certificate so he can collect on an insurance policy?"

"I know you fucking lying! Why the fuck would he think Cheno is dead? Dawson ain't did nothing for y'all."

"Granny, I had to put that lie in the streets so them niggas wouldn't go searching for my brother. It was my way of keeping him safe. That's what I said to his bum ass! He had the nerve to say he was still my daddy, and he could whoop my ass. Before I knew it, I told him I would shoot him between his eyes."

Pearl laughed until tears ran down her face. "I don't give a damn what nobody says, you were born to be a fuckin' boy. Dawson better leave my baby alone," she said, stubbing out her cigarette then picked up the remote to the TV.

"I have some money for you to put in the safe. I'll be right back."

I left to get the duffle bag from my trunk and came right back. Pearl briefly looked in my direction before focusing on the news segment on the tv. I turned to see what had her undivided attention and dropped the bag when I saw a picture of Free on the screen. Pearl increased the volume, and I couldn't believe what I heard.

"Thank you, Henry. I'm standing outside an apartment building on Howard Street where the decomposed body of a black male was found hanging in the closet. Police have identified the victim as Pierre Stewart. The case is under investigation. If anyone have any information about this crime, please contact Chicago Police."

I sat listening to the newscaster discuss more about Free and his upbringing, accomplishments, and his children. What they didn't tell was the fact his ass was a dope boy. Of course, they played a clip of his mama saying how he was an upstanding man that didn't do anything to anyone and he had no enemies.

"Pierre was a great father that loved his kids and family. He loved life and was the life of the party. When I hadn't heard from him in a few days, I went to the police to file a missing person's report. Pierre didn't go a day without calling me, so I knew something was wrong. For the police to tell me there was nothing they could do because my son was an adult, pissed me off. Now look what happened. He's dead! To say my son committed suicide is crazy. He had everything to live for and the main reason was his two kids. This was not a suicide and I want answers!"

"We've been looking for this nigga since Cheno's spot was hit. Instead of facing the consequences of his actions, he went to the other side of the city and took the easy way out."

Seeing Free's face on the screen pissed me off and I wasn't trying to hear he didn't do this shit to himself. Obviously, his mammy didn't know he had a hand in stealing from the man who fed him and his muthafuckin' kids. I didn't feel an ounce of remorse for his ass because when you live by the sword, you died by that muthafucka. Free should've went out like a G and not a weak nigga.

"There you go getting upset and not thinking shit through, Breeze. From what Cheno told me, the robbery was an inside job. Did it ever occur to you that maybe Free helped but was killed after the fact? That's what I think happen in this situation."

Ignoring what Pearl said, I took my phone out and hit Fredo's line. It rang a couple times and went to voicemail. As I was about to call him back, my phone rang with his name on display.

"Did you see the news?" I asked without saying hello.

"Nawl, what's up?"

"The police found Free on Howard. Apparently, he committed suicide. The nigga is a bitch! He helped them niggas rob my brother."

Fredo was quiet for a spell, and I thought he hung up. "Breeze, Free didn't have nothing to do with that shit. Pull up on me. I'm not discussing shit over the phone."

"I'm about to head to the hospital. Meet me there in an hour."

"Bet."

Fredo hung up and I looked at Pearl. She was sitting in deep thought before she got up from her seat with yet another cigarette between her fingers. I watched while she made her way to the kitchen causing me to follow. She stood pouring coffee in a mug.

"I'm going to call and see what information my source has for me. This shit is getting messy, and I don't want anything to happen to you in these streets. I can tell you are not going to lay low like I want you to. Think about what I said about Pierre. Cheno talked too highly of him, and I don't think he would bite the hand that fed him well. You're going to do what you want. Just be careful out there, Breeze."

"I know you're worried, and you have every right to be. It's no holds barred at this point and I'm on a mission. They don't call me Cheno's little sister for nothing. I love you, Granny. I'll call you later if I don't hear from you first."

Kissing her on the cheek, I gave Pearl a hug and left the same way I came in. The shit with Free had my mind racing. To hear Fredo and Pearl defend him had me second guessing what I thought. The truth would come out eventually, but the information I knew was accurate was the most important. Getting in my whip, I made my way to the hospital listening to Kevin Gates "In God I Trust". At this point, God got me because my protector wasn't able.

Chapter 10

Charlie

Sitting in the hospital room with Cheno, I kept looking at him hoping he would open his eyes or say something. Eating the fried fish dinner I brought with me slowly, I thought about all the years I spent with the man I thought would be my forever and cringed. Cheno was a good man who in my opinion needed attention from several women. It was something I couldn't rock with. No matter how much he proclaimed to love me, the shit was disrespectful on all levels. If I'm who his ass was with, I should've been the only woman he saw.

After leaving the club and helping air out the niggas on 15th, I made my way back to Downers Grove because I wasn't taking any chances of being followed back to Cheno's house. When I approached the door, there was a piece of paper stuck between the screen door. Glancing around, I didn't see anything on the quiet street, so I hurried inside after retrieving the note. After getting settled in, I walked into my bedroom and sat on the bed. Unfolding the paper, I smiled.

Hello, Miss Charlie.

I haven't seen you in a minute and I wanted to let you know the invitation to dinner is still on the table. A nigga is trying to get to know you. I won't push too hard, but here's

my number. Hit me up when you ready to have a night on the town with me. Shit, even a day. Your choice. Let me know.
Caesar

Caesar was persistent and it was cute, but I felt guilty by smiling at his words. Yeah, I told Cheno we were over, but he had my heart in the palm of his hand. Entertaining another was something I wasn't ready for. Plus, Cheno's words echoed in my mind and that shit alone had me shook.

I will kill any nigga I see in yo' muthafuckin face, Charlie. Don't test me. I love you. This is not the end, and we are just separated. I'm coming back for what belongs to me. Don't get too comfortable. Get yo' mind right because this shit is temporary.

He never said anything he didn't mean. But he was laid up at the moment and Caesar had my attention. I texted him and told him I'd been busy but I had his number. We've been texting ever since.

I heard a slight movement and looked over at Cheno's motionless body. He was still in the same position, so I thought I was going crazy. The text tone sounded and my attention went directly back to Caesar. Smiling wider than the Red Sea, I read his message.

Caesar: So, what are you doing right now, beautiful?"

I had yet to tell him about Cheno. With everything going on, I wasn't about to jeopardize his safety to keep the conversation going.

Me: I'm chillin' in the city at the moment. Why you ask?

Caesar: I wanna see you. Make that shit happen, ma. As a matter of fact, I'll be at your door around eight. Be ready.

That's the type of control I liked. Caesar won me over with his take charge demeanor. I was definitely going to be ready to go at eight. When I was about to respond, I heard the same sound once again and looked up. The smile fell from my lips and my eyes bulged. Cheno was staring at me with nothing but menace in his eyes. It kind of reminded me of Jack Nicholson's character in the Shining.

"You only supposed to smile like that with me," Cheno croaked out. "I damn near died and you been dick shopping."

This muthafucka been struggling to come back to the real world and the first thing he does when he opened his eyes was talk shit. Then, he had the nerve to be jealous of the thought of me conversing with someone of the opposite sex. Niggas. We stared at each other for what seemed like forever until I put my phone on the chair beside me leaning forward.

"Yes, you almost died going out in the wee hours of the morning to meet up with the bitch who had your dick down her throat at one point. But that's not my business," I said rolling my eyes. "Regardless of the fact, I've been here since the day you were brought in along with others. After the way you've been shitting on me, I didn't have to even do that, but I did. See, you would define me stepping out with another man as deception, I call it moving on with my life by any means necessary. You're worried about the wrong thing, Cheno."

Standing to my feet I walked out on his ass because his health was first priority. I went to the nurse station and informed them that Cheno was awake. We walked back into the room, and I sat back down while the nurse checked his vitals. Anger tried taking over but I blocked it because it wasn't the time to argue with him. Cheno would need all of his strength to get better.

"Mr. Woods, how are you feeling?"

"Can I get some water?" Was his reply as he looked down at his arm in the sling.

"Sure. Let me check your arm and bandages first," she said lifting the gown up. "We weren't expecting you to come out of this so soon. You did great."

"I don't feel great. My body is so sore."

"In due time, you will be good as new. It's all about healing now. Okay, I'll be right back with your water and fresh bandages. I paged the doctor, and he should be on his way up."

Cheno nodded but his eyes never left mine. Soon as the door closed behind the nurse, he groaned loudly trying to sit up on his own. The bitch in me wanted to stay put and watch his ass struggle, but the love I had for him wouldn't allow me to do it. I walked to the side of the bed and picked up the remote to the bed. I raised the upper part and helped adjust his body until he was comfortable.

"Back to that fuck shit you said before you left out of this room. If you thought me being down and out was going to mess up my state of mind, you wrong as fuck." He snarled. "I didn't go out there to be with no muthafuckin' body for one. In fact, I was trying to stop the bitch from going to twelve about you whoopin' her ass. I love you enough to not want you to go back to prison over something that was my fault. Even though you were justified in your actions, Larisa didn't think so because she wasn't trying to take that loss. She was embarrassed as hell out there after you left."

Hearing him say Larisa was going to the police made me chuckle and it felt good to know he was looking out for me at the same time. But I wasn't going to tell him that. I've been off papers for a couple years so her going to the cops wouldn't have landed me in the slammer. Can't nobody threaten me with the pigs because when I fuck you up, it won't be rewarded with jail time. Trust.

"For somebody who claims to love me, you sure as hell don't pay attention when I talk. We sat down and talked about my probation period when it ended. How the fuck do you think I was able to take the trip with you to the Bahamas the following year? See, you remember what you want to remember and that's part of your problem."

Cheno chortled lowly licking his dry lips. "Whoever the nigga is gon' get you and him fucked up in the worse way. I told you, Charlie, this shit is temporary. Any other muthafucka would be telling you to kick rocks in flip flops, but I'm not gon' even do that. Retaliation ain't the way to handle this shit, but I'm gon' let you have it. You got my permission to get yo' lick back, shawty. Tell that nigga I said don't fall in love because you won't be in his presence long."

"Cheno, hear me and hear me clearly. I left you because you didn't know how to keep your dick in your pants. You didn't appreciate me when you had me, now you want to act like I'm doing you dirty. That's cute. See, I'm not the type of woman that's going to lead you along to think I've gotten over all that you have done and stay. I respect you enough to tell you up front what it is instead of sneaking around behind your back. For the record, I don't need your permission to do a damn thang. I'm already gone," I said looking up from my phone.

While he was talking out the side of his neck, I was texting Breeze to let her know her brother was awake. She responded back promptly and that was my cue to leave his ass where he was. The nigga made it sound like he had control over what I did in life. I was going to show him better than I could tell him and his chest gon' cave in as he cried in the car. Cheno didn't realize he was about to feel exactly what I felt when he cheated on me throughout the years. The difference between what he did and what I planned to do; I was single.

"Your sister is on her way here. I'm going to leave before I say something that will hurt your feelings."

"Charlie, there's only one thing you can do to hurt me. And that is giving my pussy away. Once you do that, then you can say it's over."

Throwing the strap to my purse over my shoulder, I walked towards the door and stopped. Taking a deep breath, I turned and faced Cheno head on. The words that were about to come out of my mouth were going to set me free. I didn't hesitate another minute as I studied the sadness displayed in his eyes.

"I guess it's over."

I walked out of the hospital room and headed to the elevators. I hadn't fucked anyone since being with Cheno. It wasn't going to be easy for Caesar to get the goods because I didn't do casual sex. Cheno didn't need to know that. But I planted the seed for him to think I did.

It took me almost forty-five minutes to get through traffic to the Air BnB because there was a bad accident on the expressway. During the commute, Breeze called asking what happened between me and Cheno. I told her what transpired and she didn't have a rebuttal. After saying her brother was now her sole responsibility, I ended the call. If I was going to move on from Cheno, it had to be all or nothing. He had his way of reeling me back in, but that was not going to happen this time around. Sticking to my guns was a must.

I was sitting on the couch where I'd been since walking inside the house pondering over the slight argument me and Cheno had at the hospital. I was trying to grasp why he was so infuriated about another man when he'd been entertaining bitches for the longest time. Men couldn't take the same treatment they dished out. My body tingled nervously because in the back of my mind, I could sense something awful happening and Cheno was going to be center stage. My phone pinged and there I was smiling like a school girl with a crush when I saw Caesar's name. Opening the thread, I read his message.

Caesar: You looked exceptionally well in those leggings. I can only imagine how you're going to dress up for me for our date tonight. You're not going to flake on me, are you?

Me: Thank you and no. I'm going to take a nap first. It's been an exhausting morning. Where are we going? I don't want to be under or overly dressed.

Caesar: Casual is good. I want you to be comfortable in whatever you decide to put on. Get you some rest beautiful and I'll see you at eight.

Me: Okay, see you later.

Making my way to the bedroom, I removed my clothes and put them in the hamper by the closet. Going into the bathroom, I started the water and decided to soak for about thirty minutes to relax. Once the tub filled up, I eased my body inside and moaned, closing my eyes. The silence was too much for me to handle so I dried my hands before picking up my phone. Opening the Apple Music app "Love Song" by Kassh Paige filled the room.

I miss my cocoa butter kisses

Hope you smile when you listen

Ain't no competition, just competin' for attention

And you're like, "I'm on no games

Well, baby I been peepin' and you ain't been the same

Like, who been on your mind?

Who got yo' time?

Who you been vibin' with and why can't I make you mine?

You use to be texting me, checking me, calling me your slime

The song reminded me of all the questions I found myself asking Cheno when shit shifted and I noticed. Each time I brought my concern to his attention, I was insecure, immature, too emotional, and overreacting. It took me to leave for him to be regretful about everything he had put me through. A video I saw a few days ago online help me make the decision to walk away from Cheno completely. The guy in the video said…

You cannot heal from somebody that you are still closely attached to. A lot of us are foolish enough to believe this person that damaged me, I can heal myself by maintaining contact and allowing them to have full access. It doesn't work like that. If you truly want to heal, you gotta cut that person off. And I know it's hard.

I'm not saying it's an easy thing to do. Y'all got history, fun times, like it wasn't always all bad. But a lot of times that's what you be holding on to. Nostalgia. When in reality y'all are a long way from that intimate toxicity for a long time. You just stayed in it. Holding on and grasping at straws that used to be, and what will never be again. You gotta be honest with yourself. Do I really wanna go out there and get better? Am I cool with this? And if you cool with it, you can stay there, maintain as much contact as you want with that person. But if you truly want to heal, you gotta distance yourself.

I replayed that video ten times with tears in my eyes and knew exactly what I needed to do. Cheno waking up was a blessing and I had every intention to be by his side until he was well enough to get around on his own. My plans went out the window the moment Cheno opened his mouth in that hospital room. It has been a while since I smiled happily because of a man. Going out with Caesar was a start to living life for me and nobody else.

My energy level went down with every minute that ticked off the clock. I took the plug from the drain and turned the water on to take a shower. After washing thoroughly, I stepped out and put on the Fenty Savage robe I kept hanging on the back of the door. My bed was so inviting when I sat on it, oiling my body. Setting my alarm for six o'clock, I got under the covers and fell into a deep sleep.

***

Caesar was ringing my bell at eight o'clock on the dot. I glanced in the mirror with purse and keys in hand as I looked at my appearance one more time. The blue jean capris I wore hugged my ass like a thirsty nigga, and the peach-colored sleeveless shirt had my tatas on display for all to see. The peach stiletto heels showcased my pink French manicured toes. Applying a light coat of lip gloss, I turned off the lights and made my way to the front door. Soon as I opened it, Caesar stood looking good enough to eat with a bouquet of peach roses in hand. How ironic was it for him to pick flowers that matched my outfit with ease? I stood blushing because Cheno hadn't given me a handful of weeds since the first year of us officially being together. The thought almost made me roll my eyes and I had to check myself internally. *Bitch, this is not about Cheno! Go have a good time with this fine ass man. You only live once.*

"Hello, gorgeous. These are for you," he said, handing me the flowers.

Taking them from his hand, I gave him a quick hug and took a long whiff of his cologne. "Thank you. Let me put these in some water and I'll be ready to go. You can come in. I won't be too long."

"This place is beautiful. I thought it was being used as an Air BnB.

"It is. I'm renting it out for a few months until I can find a house I like. It's perfect for now, but I've used the layout to look for something similar," I said coming out of the kitchen drying my hands with a paper towel.

"Damn."

Caesar said lowly but not low enough that I didn't hear him.

Bypassing him, I opened the door and stood to the side. Caesar moved forward slowly but his pupils were fixated on me. It was like he was scanning my body from my feet until his gaze locked in on my face. The way he licked his lips made my kitty do a little dance in my pants. Inconspicuously, I leaned into the frame to hide the fact he had me aroused with just a glimpse.

"That nigga fucked up and pushed you into the arms of a real one. Don't worry, I'm not going to make a move on you.

Yet. I can guarantee you will be mine before you know it. With yo' sexy ass."

I chuckled and felt my cheeks grow warm under his intense stare. Caesar finally stepped out of the house and I followed closing and locked the door behind me. The smell of his cologne lingered in the air making me swoon. Caesar stood on the passenger side of his black-on-black Benz with the door open. He got another point for being a gentleman. It was always that way in the beginning stages of getting to know someone new. I wondered how long his pleasantries were going to last. *There you go with that negative shit. Enjoy your time with the man. Damn!* I checked myself again as Caesar buckled my seatbelt for me before kissing the center of my forehead.

Sitting back with a cheesy smile on my face, I reached over and pulled the handle to help Caesar gain entry. "Let me find out you've seen the movie A Bronx Tale," he said sliding into the driver seat.

"I've seen the movie, but it had nothing to do with assisting you with the door."

"Yeah, okay. Don't let me find out down the line you a street princess. I can't say what I'd do if you decide to up a blick on me. Wait, did you injure your ex before you left him?"

Caesar's statement caught me off guard causing me to look at his ass with a side eye glare. Cheno had just come out of the coma and we didn't know exactly who was involved in his shooting. The hairs on the back of my neck stood tall and I automatically reached behind me to rub the feeling away.

"I'm bullshitting with you, girl. Stop being so serious." He laughed. "I have a question though. Do you know how to shoot a gun?"

"What's with the gun questions, Caesar? My demeanor doesn't even scream ride or die. Far as my ex, we parted ways on good terms. There's nothing in this world that would make me do bodily harm to a nigga because his actions didn't meet my expectations. I don't know what type of females you are used to dealing…"

"I was joking, Charlie. I apologize for causing you discomfort and bringing up your ex. The situation between y'all is obviously still fresh and I was out of line. One thing for sure, I don't want this to ruin the night I have planned for us. Okay?"

"I'm cool. Just don't do that right now. Maybe one day I'll be able to joke around in that manner. This isn't the day," I said turning towards the window. "Are you ready to tell me where we're going?"

"I wanted it to be a surprise, but I've rubbed you the wrong way so I have some making up to do. There's a new restaurant that opened a couple months ago downtown and I wanted to check it out."

"You talking about Brisco's?"

"Yeah. One of my colleagues recommended the place. He said it's really nice."

"I was going to suggest going there with my girls. Now, I can see if it's all the reviews hyped it up to be firsthand," I replied. "How were you able to get reservations? They were booked for weeks according to the information on the website."

"I actually know the owner and he was able to do me a solid." Caesar smirked as he glanced over at me.

His skin was the color of milk chocolate and appeared just as smooth without any blemishes. When he smiled, his teeth gleamed every time the light bounced off them. Caesar was finer than wine and I'm quite sure he knew that too. My usual go to was light skinned men but there was something about him that had me wanting to get to know more about him. I had to remind myself to play his ass close because of the little jokey joke he called himself saying a few moments prior. Caesar interrupted my thoughts when he started speaking about the very thing I was thinking about.

"There is so much I want to know about the woman I've come to admire with ease. A cozy dinner for two will allow us to do just that. Get to know one another. Plus, it seems I've taken a first from your bucket list and hope there are many more to come."

"You sure did. Smooth as hell too. If the food isn't good, this will be our first and last date."

"Damn, it's like that? I'm not the chef though. How you gon' hold me accountable for their fuck up?" he quizzed.

"But you chose the spot." I laughed. "The way this plays out between us is determined by the service and quality of Brisco's. Your homie better come correct because you are on the verge of fumbling, my dude."

"That's not fair but I'm gon' let you have it, beautiful. By the way, you look good tonight."

"Thank you." I blushed. "You don't look too shabby yourself."

Sitting back taking in the sights, the interior of the vehicle became deathly silent. Caesar hit the power button on the radio and Kems "I Can't Stop Loving You" flowed through the speakers.

I can't stop loving you. I can't help myself. And I can't get over you. No matter what I tell myself.

The song was one I played on repeat whenever Cheno did something stupid. I'd contemplate leaving then ended up staying for the bullshit to continue. Tears would be the result of the lyrics. Not that night. I was actually able to enjoy the music with a smile. Caesar exited the expressway and I became excited the closer we got to the restaurant. Pulling in front of the establishment, it seemed as if Brisco's were closed. With a look of confusion, I turned to Caesar.

"I thought you made reservations. This place looks closed for the night."

"It's closed to the public. I rented out the place for a few hours," Caesar explained.

I was shocked beyond belief. No man had ever shut down a spot for me. Caesar was starting to appear like an "it's too good to be true" type of situation. Once again, he was walking around the car to open the door for me. I hadn't even noticed he was no longer inside the car. That's how hard I was fixated on the fact the man had arranged for a popular restaurant to be closed to the public for a date. Caesar held my hand as I exited the vehicle, placing the other onto the small of my back. Even in heels, he towered over me. An employee met us at the entrance, ushering us inside.

"Good evening, Caesar. Ma'am. Welcome."

I nodded a hello with a smile.

"Good evening to you too. Everything's set up according to my requests?"

"Of course. Follow me. I'm Alex and I'll be your server for the night. Anything you may need, I'm here to make sure you all receive."

The restaurant was eloquently decorated and very classy. There were teardrop chandeliers hanging from the ceiling, the tables were draped in black and crème table cloths, and crystal dinnerware. The walls were beautiful as well. They were black with Crème abstracts and a lot of African American art hanging throughout. Whoever owned Brisco's did a phenomenal job with the décor.

Alex led us into what I assumed was a private room that was used for parties. The moment I entered I was in awe. Caesar had the same peach rose petals as the bouquet he had given me earlier scattered about the room. What truly warmed my heart was the words, 'One day you will be mine' in the middle of the floor. Caesar's jokes were forgotten immediately.

"Oh, you laying it on thick, thick." I chuckled as Caesar hugged me from behind.

"Anything for you, beautiful."

Pulling out the chair for me to sit, Caesar rounded the table to take his seat in front of me. I continued to look around the room as I listened to the artist Sade's voice croon through the sound system. I was only familiar with her music because Breeze and Cheno would listen to her whenever they missed their mother. She was a huge fan. "Cherish the Day" was one I knew all too well and I liked it.

I cherish the day
I won't go astray
I won't be afraid
You won't catch me running
You're ruling the way that I move
You take my air

"This is a beautiful restaurant. Who owns this place? They put a lot of thought into every design." I said as Alex walked in with a bottle of *Dom Pérignon* champagne.

"I agree. It took him a few years to come up with a plan of what he thought the people would love. He nailed it." he grinned. "I believe his name is Caesar Brisco. If I'm not mistaken."

My mind was working slower than usual so I didn't pick up what he said at first. Then it hit me. "You own this place?"

Caesar nodded taking a sip from his glass. "Why didn't you just say you were taking me to your restaurant?"

"Where is the fun in that? I wanted to see your take firsthand and your reaction was priceless. I promise I wasn't trying to be secretive. You would've been informed at some point during this date."

"I can respect that. Well, you did the damn thing. Congratulations," I said holding my glass up to toast with him. "Tell me more about you, Caesar."

"Where do I start. As you know, I am Twenty-nine years young, no kids, and single. I was born and raised in Pittsburg, Pennsylvania along with my two brothers. My older brother died at the age of twenty-eight by gun violence. Today he would've been thirty-six if he was still alive. That was my dude and I miss him." Caesar cleared his throat before continuing. "Anyway, I moved to Illinois five years ago and decided to stay and open Brisco's II. There's a Brisco's back home in Pittsburg. It is doing well too. I'm proud of myself actually."

"That's what's up! I'm proud of you too. Working hard pays off," I said honestly. "What did you do before you opened your first restaurant?"

"I graduated from the University of Pittsburg with a degree in business at the age of twenty-one and my grandmother presented me with a check for two hundred thousand dollars. She had the money sitting in the bank since my older brother's death. My grandma went through a time when she lost her grandson and daughter. She tried her best to keep me out the streets. That only lasted until she took her last breath three years later. Hustling became something I did to keep my mind off my granny being gone. With that money my granny gave me and the cash I'd saved from hustling, I put my business plan from college to the test and opened Brisco's at twenty-three. It wasn't an easy task, but I made that shit work."

The way Caesar explained his journey was sad but impressive. Being so young with ambitions was hard for an experienced entrepreneur I could only imagine the restless nights he endured in the process. Caesar pulled it off making a name for himself. I had a few questions for him, but I didn't want to sour the evening asking about the people who was no longer alive to witness his success. Instead, I kept my questions solely on his business.

"Why aren't you advertising Brisco's as *your* place of business? I thought a white man owned this restaurant. There's nothing like another successful brother doing the damn thing and getting recognition from a job well done."

"I don't need all the glam that comes along with my accomplishments. A low profile is the best way to go coming from the shit I had to go through in life. As long as the proceeds are hitting my account, that's all I'm worried about."

"What are you hiding from, Caesar?" I asked seriously.

"I'm not hiding from anything. I call it blending in," he said sipping from his glass. Alex entered with a cart filled with covered plates and I wondered how he knew what I wanted to eat. Caesar must've saw the expression on my face because he explained.

"I took the liberty of preordering for us. I hope you don't mind. If there's anything you want, order it."

Alex placed a seafood boil, a bowl of rice with vegetables, and two steaks, on the table. I had no complaints because my fuck up the food meter was on full charge. One thing I hadn't come back from was eating like I was still in prison. Securing the napkin around my neck, I was ready. I added a little bit of rice and vegetables to a plate then dug into the seafood boil. Caesar was watching me in amazement but that didn't stop me. I wiped my mouth and took a breath.

"You better eat before I eat your share too."

"Damn, you ain't got no shame in eating. Most females pick at their food trying to be all cute and shit while their food gets cold."

"I was…" I almost slipped and revealed I served time, but I caught myself. "I was raised with brothers who would steal my food. I haven't taught myself how to slow down at my big age. Plus, this food is good as hell."

"I'm glad you're enjoying it. Luck was on my side because I can have another shot at making you my woman."

Caesar was moving a bit fast for my liking. We had met weeks ago but tonight was the first time we had gone out on a date. Being anything other than a friend wasn't happening anytime soon. He may be able to graduate to a friend with benefits, but that wasn't in the near future either. One thing about me, I had to be comfortable with a man before I took a major step. We weren't at that stage at all.

"It's going to take several shots to be honest. I appreciate you going all out for this date, but it only advanced you a couple notches into friendship. You know the situation I just got out of."

"Actually, I don't. How about you tell me a little more about it." Caesar steepled his hands together as he stared at me intensely.

"My past relationship is one I don't want to go in depth with. To make a long story short, I gave him my all for years and he didn't know how to stop playing in the field. He had everything he needed at home and still needed the attention of rats to make him happy. So, I left. End of story. Rushing anything with you will only cause me to use you to make him jealous and I'm not on that." I shrugged as I picked up another king crab and cracked the shell.

"I admire your honesty, Charlie. Being a rebound nigga is something I've never been and have no intentions of playing the role. When I have my eyes set on something, I usually get what I want. That something is you. Giving up isn't an option for me."

Caesar stood to his feet while wiping his hands on the black cloth. When he walked out of the room, my phone buzzed in my purse. I cleaned my hands to see who was texting me.

My Love: Wya?

Me: Minding my business. What do you want, Cheno?

My Love: You are my business. Now, where the fuck are you?

Cheno was out of his mind questioning me like he had the right to do so. One would think with him just coming out of a coma, he would be resting. Not his hardheaded ass, he was worrying about the very thing he took for granted. Now he wanted to do checkups. If he wanted to know where I was, he would have to find out on his own. But I had no problem sharing what I was doing.

Me: I'm on a date. Anything else?

My Love: Have your fun while I'm down. If you still fuckin' with this nigga when I get back up, I'm turning his world upside down. Enjoy the rest of your night, ma.

Me: You got your nerve! At least I didn't lie to you. I left your ass before I allowed someone else to pursue me. You were entertaining any and everybody and got the nerve to be mad! Fuck you, Cheno!

I was mad as hell because how could he threaten somebody's life after what he had done for years. I knew he was probably typing out a long ass message so I put my phone back in my purse. After five minutes, he still hadn't replied and I was kind of nervous. Cheno wasn't the type of man to let something go that easily. He couldn't make anything shake from the hospital bed he was still lying in, but that didn't mean he wasn't conjuring up a plan.

This was the reason I didn't want to take things further with Caesar. It would put him smack dab in the middle of my bullshit and I didn't want to be responsible for what happened to him. Sitting quietly waiting for Caesar to return, I tried to eat a little bit more and no longer had an appetite. The text from Cheno changed my entire mood in just a few minutes. Turning toward the entryway as I heard movement, Caesar was entering with bags and packages in hand. Behind him Alex was walking with the biggest bouquet I'd ever seen.

"Caesar, what is all of this?" I asked in amazement.

"When I told you I always get what I want, I wasn't just talking. These gifts are for you, beautiful."

I observed the gifts Caesar held but I didn't move an inch. Alex held the flowers out to me and I didn't reach to take them from him. The room was silent. My inability to move as if I was paralyzed frightened me. As I kept my eye on Caesar, I believed he noticed my discomfort to his gift presentation. There were consequences to accepting lavish presents from a man who you saw as just a friend. Caesar was foreseeing the two us being together as a couple and I wasn't on the same page as him.

"Alex, place those on the table over there," Caesar pointed across the room. "You can clear the food and package it up if you may. I need to talk with Miss Charlie privately."

His eyes bore into mine and I shifted in my seat. I broke contact focusing on the Alex as he piled the dishes on a cart. When he left the room, Caesar sat the bags he held in front of me on the table. He pulled a chair next to me. Sitting with his legs apart, he moved me closer to him.

"What's on your mind?" he asked softly grasping my hand.

"Thank you for thinking of me but I can't accept any of this," I replied lowering my head. Caesar used his finger and lifted my chin so I was looking directly at him. "I'm not going to lead you to believe there's a chance for us to be anything more than friends. In this day in time, that shit is dangerous."

"Charlie, I don't do nothing with ill intensions. This was what I wanted to do for you because I know all you have been through lately can be very depressing. You may appear as if you're alright on the outside, but I know on the inside you're beyond hurt. Buying you these things were only to make you smile for the moment and to let you know you are worthy. I want you to go with the flow and allow me to keep seeing you glow. Can you do that?"

"I can go with the flow as friends. I can't promise you anything more."

I retrieved my purse taking my phone out. Going to the Lyft app, I quickly requested a car unbeknownst to him. The driver was two minutes away and I was relieved. Caesar reached over and grabbed the bags. He placed them on the floor handing me a small gift bag from Pandora. I refused to take it because I already explained why. Instead of forcing me to do so, he opened it revealing the bracelet inside. My phone ting notified me that my ride was outside.

"I'm sorry, Caesar but I have to go," I said standing to my feet. "Thank you for a great night."

Standing to my feet, I walked out and left him sitting there in confusion. There was no way I could give Caesar what he wanted so I had to leave him and his gifts behind.

Chapter 11

Cheno

Doctors were coming in and out of my room from the moment I came out of the coma. They were doing their job by making sure everything was good with me, but I wanted them to get the fuck out. My mind was on Charlie and the little date she was on. She claimed the loyalty she had for me was strong but was out entertaining a nigga. I know, that was the wrong shit to think about, nonetheless, it was bothering me. The only thing I wanted was to get out of the hospital so I could get my woman back. Wasn't no breaking up. Me and Charlie was forever.

"Mr. Woods, you are one lucky man. This ordeal could've been tragic for you. By the grace of God, you are here today," The doctor said cutting into my thoughts. "We are going to keep you for observation for a couple days to make sure you are totally fine to go home."

"What's your definition of a couple of days?"

"Three to four days at the most," he replied.

"That's not going to work for me. I'm ready to go home now. I'll give y'all one more day then, I'm out. I can lay in my own bed comfortably with my relatives watching over me. I don't need to be here for that to happen. All I need from you is to have my discharge papers printed and ready for me to leave this muthafucka bright and early in the morning."

As I finished my statement, the door opened and Breeze entered with Fredo right behind her. The doctor turned and smiled greeting my sister. With his hand outstretched, he started trying to convince her into talking me out of leaving.

"Miss Woods, it's good to see you. I was just telling Ricky that it would be wise for him to stay here for observations. He's adamant about going home tomorrow."

"Ayo, doc, I know you think you know what's best for me. However, snitching to my little sister isn't going to help you much. Long as I'm not leaving under life-or-death circumstances, you can't hold me in this muthafucka against my will. Now, I done already told you what it is. After today, I will no longer be a patient under yo' care. As a matter of fact, go get a head start on that paperwork and don't forget the prescription for pain medication. You can leave."

Breeze stood glaring at me the same way my mama used to do when she didn't agree with my decisions. The doctor decided not to argue his point and left the room quietly. Fredo cleared his throat walking closer to the bed. I was sitting up with my phone lying on my lap face down as I waited for him to say something.

"Nigga, what?" I barked.

"Who you been on the phone with?"

Tilting my head to the side to figure out who the fuck he was talking to. "I'm the wrong one for you to be trying to lil girl. I'm a whole muthafuckin' man around this bitch!"

"Cheno, you need to calm yo' ass down. He asked you a simple question and you going off the deep end." Breeze snapped. "It's important for you to answer the question because we got muthafuckas thinking you didn't make it out of this shit."

"Why the fuck would y'all throw dirt on me like that when I'm alive and well?"

"Nigga, are you slow or stupid? You were shot and left for dead! The muthafuckas that did the shit is still free as a bird and was waiting for word to finish the job! What the fuck could you do while laid up in a coma to protect yourself? Not a damn thang. It was to protect yo' simple minded ass. Now, I'm asking you, who have you called?"

Breeze was mad but I also saw the hurt in her eyes. My sister looked like she hadn't slept for days and that alone unruffled my feathers. She stepped forward and all I saw was myself in her stance. The way she bored into my soul without saying anything had me settling down to answer the question that was asked.

"I've only talked to Charlie. Well, I texted her." I paused. "Do you know about the nigga she's seeing?"

"That shit is between you and her. I have better shit to think about than Charlie riding another nigga's dick. It's about time she chose herself."

"What the fuck?" I scowled.

"Brah, you worried about the wrong shit! Put that shit on the back burner for now. Free is dead," Breeze said changing the subject.

When I didn't say nothing, I could feel both of them burning the side of my face. "I know he's dead. Free didn't have shit to do with what happened at the trap."

"Hol' up! How you know that?" Fredo asked. "You haven't been out of this hospital. Wait, Charlie told you. I was about to say."

"Charlie didn't tell me shit! Don't mention her name if y'all ain't gon' tell me about the nigga she out there with."

"Okay, so if Charlie didn't tell you, who did?"

I had to think about how I was going to explain the how to them. The last thing I needed was my sister signing papers to have my ass committed. The shit I went through while in the coma still baffled me. So, I knew they were going to think I was crazier than a bitsy bug. Breeze sat down and crossed her foot over her knee as he waited. Positioning myself comfortably against the pillows to stall for time, I shook my head slowly.

"What I'm about to say may seem farfetched to y'all but it's my truth. Hear me out and don't say nothing until I'm done."

I ran down everything I endured from the talk with my mama, to the electrical shocks that flowed through my body. When I told them where Free was found, both of their eyes were bucked. Fredo's mouth was hanging open so wide I could see his tonsils. He had to sit on the edge of the bed before his legs gave out.

"That bitch Larisa was right there with those niggas and it was a muthafucka named Lord who shot me. Tank's bitch ass called the hit. They are set up on 15th and Trumbell. I need y'all to roll on them niggas soon as possible."

"I already took care of that," Breeze said nonchalantly.

"About that," Fredo directed his words at her. "Didn't I ask you to hold off on that before y'all even went out? How did you end up on 15th?"

"That shit was unavoidable. Letty and her wannabe tough ass sisters tried to jump Honey at the club. I wasn't letting that shit ride. The law was coming so we followed them hoes wherever they went. It just so happened they went to 15th. Instead of following the bitch, I let her think we turned off and left. Then lit that muthafucka up. At that point, I didn't give a fuck who got hit. I just wanted blood."

"Well, you killed Lord. That's a plus. But that shit could've went far left."

"I didn't see y'all making moves. Somebody had to set that shit off." Breeze snapped back. "I could've lost my brother behind them."

"Breeze, you are on a rampage. You already killed Sia."

"Sia? What the fuck she do?" I asked.

"She wouldn't tell me where to find Larisa. She wanted to be loyal to her *friend* therefore, I made her stand on that shit. Knowing her snake ass, Sia knew Larisa was butt hurt and was going to set you up. The bitch had to go. Simple."

"I'm with Fredo. You need to pipe that shit down, sis. I'm out of here tomorrow and in a few days, it's on. I'm gon' find out who helped that nigga Tank with this shit."

Breeze rolled her eyes and sat back.

"I already know who helped him," Fredo said. "It was Sketty."

"Sketty?"

"Yup. Quell and Lil Mike tailed that nigga because he was acting weird when he pulled up at the trap. He was late but that's not what put me on alert. The first thing he wanted to know was if we had any leads on who shot you. The nigga was shifting his eyes, swinging his arms, and wouldn't look at me. That shit was a red flag because his body language told me he didn't give a fuck, he just needed the information. I smelled bullshit from the gate."

I listened closely to what he said and I couldn't believe Sketty was the snake in the grass. He used to work at the carwash I owned and was a hard worker. He had four kids with four different females and they all was giving him the blues because he couldn't afford to take care of his kids the way he should. The shit was killing him on a daily basis but he kept pushing.

Sketty was arrested for failing to pay his child support while he was at work. Being the man that I am, I got him a lawyer to help fight the case. In addition, I paid his back child support and offered him a higher position. Instead of accepting the position, Sketty asked me to put him on my team. Usually, I wouldn't just bring a nigga in my organization, but I trusted him. It was damn near a year before I put Sketty on. He proved himself in every way imaginable. Sketty was one of my top workers and was able to keep up with his payments and improved his life tremendously. I never thought he would be involved with trying to kill me. I couldn't think of one reason why I was targeted. There were so many questions running through my mind and only Sketty had the answers.

"To make a long story short, Sketty's been feeding Tank information. That's why we kept the fact of you being alive within a tight circle. He had been asking questions at the trap but nobody could tell him what he wanted to know because they didn't know shit. To be honest, the homies are grieving your death too and I feel bad for keeping them out of the loop. I can't trust nobody until we get at everybody that's involved in this shit."

The more I listened, the madder I became. My hands were balled into fists and I wanted to sign myself out of the hospital right then and there. Muthafuckas thought I was a bitch ass nigga but they were going to find out I'm not the one to play with. After my mama died, I fell back from the stupid shit. At that point, I didn't give a fuck. I was ready to chop the heads off every snake that hissed at me.

"Where Sketty at now?" I asked.

"I haven't seen him. Lil Mike called the other day saying Sketty was at the trap. He made a couple sales and by the time I arrived, he had left."

"This shit is a punch in the gut. I helped that nigga. You know what? That shit don't even matter. Sketty gon' get what's coming to him right along with Cheese and Tank. I got some calls to make and once I have a plan, I'll fill you in on it. In the meantime, play that nigga close. What's going on with Cheese and Tank?"

Fredo frowned at Breeze. "15th street is shut down. That was the only spot I know about."

"Yo' you act like I fucked shit up. Nah, I did what I was supposed to do and that was stand on muthafuckin' business. But check this out. Y'all may not agree with what I'm about to say. There's only one person who can put eyes on Cheese at this time."

Already knowing where Breeze thought process was, I shook my head no.

"Cheno, hear me out before you shut down my idea. Cheese still wants Honey. We can use her to get at him."

"Man, you crazy as hell. I'm not putting her in harm's way. Honey just spent ten years of her life behind bars and you want her to possibly get jammed up again? Nah, I'm not with that shit, Breeze."

"Don't underestimate what Honey is capable of, Cheno. She can pull this off."

The door opened just as Breeze finished what she was saying. Quell walked in holding Honey's hand. Seeing the two of them together had me feeling like a proud big brother. I couldn't even voice that because the way Quell glowered at Breeze let me know he heard part of what she suggested.

"Honey, can pull off what, sis?" he asked.

Breeze stood up reacting on Quell's demeanor. That's one of the traits I hated she had because Breeze didn't back down from nobody. No matter who it was.

"I was telling them since Cheese has gone into hiding, the only way to get at him is through Honey."

"He ain't about to agree with that shit. You wasting yo' time explaining it to him." I barked.

"First and foremost," Honey said cutting in. "I'm standing right here. I can speak for myself. Cheno, for the record, Quell is not my man nor my daddy. He can never tell me what to do. Just so y'all know, Cheese has already bitten the bait. Leave his ass to me."

Quell's jaw clenched forcefully. He was visibly upset by what Honey revealed. It was obvious they hadn't made anything official between them. He smashed because my cousin was glowing and I noticed the pep in her step. When they walked in hand in hand, I knew what was up. Quell wasn't the type of man that bounced from woman to woman. When he hit, he staked claim. And in his mind, Honey was his.

"Honey, don't play with me. You know what's up," Quell said calmly. "At what point have you been communicating with this muthafucka?"

147

"Take the hostility out your voice. I'm not like any female you've ever dealt with in the past. Save all that macho shit for them hoes in Texas. I don't play that dominant stuff in public." She smirked.

Quell matched her expression keeping his cool. Them two muthafuckas were talking in a sex language only they understood. I peeped that shit and sniggered lowly. Freaky asses.

"However, Cheese hit me in my social media inbox the night I beat Letty and her sister's ass at the club. He wanted me to leave the situation alone. Then in the next breath, he voiced how sorry he was for not being there for me. Blah, blah, blah. When he started talking about how much he missed and still loved me, I knew he wasn't bothered about what happened to you, Cheno. My mind automatically went to the deceitful bitches I was locked up with. I didn't trust them and I didn't believe a word Cheese called himself professing. So, I played his ass the same way he was trying to do me. Quell, you have nothing to worry about. Cheese will never get any of my nookie. He may see it, and even smell it, but that's about all. Pussy is power and it's going to be Cheese's downfall."

"I'm not with this shit, Honey. You know what I told you. It's powerful and it belongs to me," Quell stated addressing the elephant in the room. "I can't tell you what to do. I know how you coming behind yo' family. Let me find out and that's yo' ass! At least I know what I'm up against with this issue. You better kill this muthafucka in the most gruesome way too. Ain't no fuckin' going on either!"

It was up to me to reassure Honey's safety. Cheese wasn't going to be on a friendship type of deal with her. He was definitely gonna want to fuck. I had to make sure Honey understood the position she was putting herself in for revenge. It was a dangerous game and she needed to be ready for whatever may happen.

"Honey, you have to make sure your mind is not solely on get back. You need to have a level head in order to make this shit believable when it comes to Cheese. Trust me, he's going to be watching your body language closely because he already violated your family in the worse way."

"I can handle myself. Y'all already know what this man put me through. I'm going to allow him to think he's making up for ten years of neglect, but there's no coming back from what he put me through. Not to mention, he had a hand in trying to eliminate the person who rode with me throughout the bid I took for his ass."

"You're too emotional. I don't think you should so this, Honey. Straight up. Your mind is made up and the last thing I want is for you to go out and handle this shit on your own." I turned to Quell. "Bro, I'll make sure she's covered at all times. I'm making some calls and we will have some silent killers on our side soon."

"I got that covered. My guys from Georgia touched down a couple hours ago. A few of them will be on security detail posted up at her business and wherever the fuck she goes."

"That's what the fuck I'm talking about. Honey, you cool with that?"

"I don't mind at all. Long as they secure and not interfere, I don't mind them protecting me. They have to be conspicuous though. Meaning, they can't roll around in the same whips all the time. That will tip Cheese off and we don't know what type of people he has watching his back. Even though I believe he's going to make sure no one knows he's spending time with me. We have to keep in mind, Cheese has a woman."

Quell still wasn't feeling the fact of Honey being in on the plan. He grabbed her hand before opening the door and escorted her out. Breeze watched as they left in confusion. Me on the other hand understood how Quell felt in that moment. My sister didn't dwell too long before she put her attention back on me.

"What you got for me?" she asked. "I'm not sitting this out so don't even part your lips to say it. Unlike Honey, I'll take matters into my own hands."

Protect your sister from the streets, Cheno. It's bad enough you're in them. I don't want that for Breeze.

Closing my eyes, I silently apologized to my mama and prayed in the same breath. Hopefully what I was about to do didn't backfire on me. There was no way I could tell her to allow me to handle this shit without her. I blame myself because I'd pulled Breeze in on beef in the past and I had no choice except to let her get down.

"You are not to make a move without me. I will be the person who informs you of what's going on."

"I smell bullshit. I'm telling you now, Cheno. Don't try to lil nigga me. I'm not one of your workers. I will square up with yo' ass. Hell, if push comes to shove, I will be the one to take you out."

I nodded in agreement because I wasn't in the mood to argue with her. Fredo was standing against the wall witnessing the banter from Breeze. I knew she would never hurt me for real, but her threats could cut deep. Bypassing my sister, I needed to know where Fredo's head was with all the shit that was going on. I couldn't read him for some reason and that had never happened in all the years we'd been friends.

"Fredo, what's your thoughts?" I asked.

"To be honest, now that you are awake and alright, I want to tear this muthafuckin' city up. If I had it my way, the politicians in Chicago would be out of millions from the damage I have in mind. But I'm going to follow yo' lead. Honey's role is one I don't agree with. The only thing I know about her is through you. You sure she can deal with this?"

I sat wondering myself if my cousin was capable. "Yeah, she's going to be good. I have faith in her because she's not the same kid that went away in her teenage years. Prison hardens most men and I can only imagine what the system does to women. Honey came out unscathed and is not using being away as an excuse. It has a lot to do with the support she had while inside and the help I provided when she got out. The way she murders Cheese will tell me if she needs to be evaluated or not." Breeze laughed loudly.

"Honey won't need to be evaluated. Her hatred for Cheese runs deep and you know this. It's been a long time coming for her to get back at him and I'm here for it. His bitch gon' be found stankin' too. I'll put money on it. Don't underestimate Honey. While we talking about it, you better check on her mama too because if I was Honey, Vickie's ass would get it too."

"Breeze, shut yo' ass up. I'm trying to be serious and you talking about the girl killing her own mama."

"You act like I'm lying or some shit." She cackled sitting back as I scowled at her angrily.

"Fredo, I need you to do me a solid. Take twenty racks to Miss Tina and call me when you're on your way so I can call her. We gotta help with Free's homegoing to make sure he's laid to rest in the right way.

"I got you. I'm gon' head out to take care of that now then. Do you need me to come pick you up tomorrow?"

"Yup, because I gotta work at nine. His ass don't fuck with me like that no way. It would be best for you to come get him before I push his ass on the expressway while the car is moving." Breeze responded.

"Be easy on my bro." Fredo laughed. "I'm glad you back, Cheno. Now you just gotta heal, nigga."

"One day at a time. That's all I got for you, but my injuries will not stop me from handling business. Hit me up when you're on your way to Tina's."

Fredo left and I picked up my phone to call the first person on my list. Stalling over the contact I went to; I was hesitant to press it because the tongue lashing I was bound to receive was going to be brutal. Miss Pearl wasn't going to hide how she really felt about me being shot. It wasn't my fault and I couldn't predict the future. One couldn't tell her that shit though. Looking up when I heard movement, I forgot Breeze was still in the room.

"Why are you still here?" I asked.

"I was going to wait until you finished your calls to talk with you. There's one more thing I want to tell you."

"Okay, what is it?"

"Dawson called my phone because he heard you were killed."

"So, now the nigga care, huh?" I laughed. "It takes a nigga to die for him to reach out. He's a joke."

"Nah, he don't give a fuck about either one of us. Yo' daddy wanted me to send him a copy of the death certificate so he could give it to the insurance company. He had to get my number from Nicki in order to call me with that bullshit."

"I've taken care of us since the day he walked the fuck out of our lives and all he did was pay for an insurance policy on my life. The nigga ain't shit and was sitting back waiting for me to die so he could cash in."

"Everything you said, I mentioned to his deadbeat ass. I also said I wouldn't put it past him if he had one on mama too. Dawson is going to be a thorn in my ass, Cheno. I'm letting you know now; I will kill his ass then help the family look for the body."

"I know you will, sis. If he contacts you again, let me handle that. Is his number still the same?"

"Yup. You can't call him though because you're dead, remember?"

"I'm aware. It doesn't mean I'll be in this position forever. Dawson will dig a hole for himself deep enough to get trapped in. He's still the same ain't shit nigga we've known all our lives. I hope you gon' be ready to handle yo' daddy if the time arises."

"Shid, I don't have to wait for him to put his foot in his mouth. I'll find him today and put him out his misery like a rabid animal."

I couldn't do nothing but laugh because Breeze was dead serious. She couldn't stand Dawson's ass. Somebody could offer her a million dollars to be nice to him for a day and she would turn that shit down. Watching as she stood and hiked up her pants, I knew she was about to head out. My mind went back to Charlie and I had to ask the question that had been bugging me since she told me about her little date.

"Aye, Breeze. Who is the nigga Charlie fucking with?"

"If I knew I would tell you. But since I don't, mind ya business bro. You fumbled and that's something you have to live with from this day forward," she said hunching her shoulder. "Don't go making that girl's life miserable."

"You know me so well, sis. That's exactly what I'm going to do. Charlie knows it's us against the world. But I want you to be safe out there. Activate the eyes in the back of your head and in your ears."

"I'm alert at all times. I was trained by the best even though his ass is doubting my abilities. I love you, bro. I'll see you when I leave the shop tomorrow."

"I love you too, sis."

I watched my sister leave and hoped like hell she didn't get into no shit. Breeze could only compose herself for so long. Hearing that Dawson reached out for the sole purpose of financial gain blew the fuck out of me. I couldn't wait for the day I got to read his ass his rights. Putting all that shit to the back burner, I went back to my phone and hit the call button. Miss Pearl answered on the first ring.

"Breeze, why are you calling me on Cheno's phone?"

"Because it's not Breeze," I replied. The line was silent for all of three seconds before she screamed loudly in my ear.

"Cheno! Praise God! You don't know how happy I am to hear your voice. I told your sister you were going to be alright!" Pearl sniffled.

"No crying, granny. I'm alright and thank you for praying for me. I heard and felt every word. I love you so much."

"I know you do. Enough of this crying shit. Cheno, how the hell you allow coochie to cloud your judgement?"

"That's not what happened, granny." I laughed. "Larisa was threatening to send Charlie to jail. I couldn't allow that to happen. The more she called and texted talking shit, the angrier I became. My plan was to sweet talk her and do something to her. I didn't make it to my destination."

"Okay, so you were protecting Charlie. That's all good but now we need to make this shit right. I talked to Grant…"

"You talking about G from the Goon Squad?" I quizzed.

"Yup. I have spoken with G and Scony about what happened to you. They will be giving you a call sometime today because I'm about to inform them that you are awake. Shit is about to get real, Cheno. You know they don't play games in these streets."

Grant Davenport and Demarious Jones had the streets shook back in the day when Scony's lil cousin Malikhi was killed. Folks still talked about how they painted the city red without ever serving a day in prison. I'd had a talk or two with both of them when I first took over the southside, but it wasn't like we were friends or no shit like that. To hear they were going to step in to help with my situation was an honor. Most niggas would reject the offer. Not me, I knew my soldiers weren't strong enough to handle what we were up against. I didn't think I needed that kind of manpower because I didn't have beef. How wrong was I?

"Oh, I know. Make that call. I'm quite sure you already know what they're going to say. But I'll be waiting."

"They will tell you all you need to know. I'll talk to you later, baby."

Pearl hung up before I could respond. I took that time to order something to eat but wished like hell I'd told somebody to bring me something from the outside. Some hospital food had no seasoning and was dry as fuck. Looking over the menu, I chose a chicken sandwich and fries with a Sprite. I regretted that shit the moment I placed the order. It was the only choice I had or I'd have to listen to my gut talking to me until I was released the next day. My phone chimed and I received a text from Fredo.

Fredo: I got the money together and I'm on my way to Miss Tina's house.

Me: Bet. Thanks man

Taking a deep breath, I dialed the number of Free's mom. I waited for her to answer and was ready to hang up as the phone rang. Removing the device from my ear, I heard a faint voice on the other end and hurried to speak.

"Hello?" I spoke.

"Cheno, is that you?" she asked surprised.

"Yeah, ma. It's me."

"I heard you were dead! I'm——"

"Ma, listen to me. Do not tell anyone that you talked to me. I just learned what happened to Free. The people that killed him are the same folks that shot me. I promise they will be taken care of. I'm sorry about what happened to my homie. Fredo is on his way to you right now. I know money will not ease the pain of losing your son, my brother, but I want to make sure he is laid to rest in the best manner possible."

"You're right. It will not bring Free back, but it will help me in the long run. I have insurance to cover the funeral. I knew my son didn't commit suicide. I'm grateful that you thought of me. There have been many mothers where the so-called friends only came by to pay their respects. I'm lucky that my son had a real one by his side. Far as keeping you being alive a secret, I will never put you in harm's way. In my big age, I still don't fuck with the police and would rather you get justice for my son."

I told Miss Tina I would be to see her soon and ended the call. The hurt in her voice was something I couldn't continue to listen to. My objective was to tell her about the money I had for her. The guilt of thinking Free was against me ate me alive. It shouldn't have been a thought in my mind if he was behind the robbery. But one couldn't trust anybody when money was involved. As the saying goes, money was the root of all evil. My nigga just didn't allow that shit to come between us. It costed him his life and that shit was far worse to me now that I knew the truth.

As I waited for my food, I went onto social media under a fake account and went to Larisa's page. I scrolled reading all of her posts and one from two days prior caught my attention.

I can't believe the love of my life was taken from me! Lord you were everything I ever wanted and I had you for six whole years. The westside will not be the same without you. We gon' get the niggas that did this to you baby. I promise. I'm not ready to say goodbye. Save a spot for me and I'll see you soon.

Reading that shit had me laughing like I was at a Katt Williams comedy show. Larisa was a joke because the bitch wasn't thinking about her nigga when my pipe was down her throat. After the first time I smashed, she was moaning she loved me. Females were the most deceptive creatures on earth. Us men were dogs too, but that shit took the cake. She didn't have to worry because she would see Lord again sooner than she expected.

I went to my page and was instantly pissed. The posts I was tagged in gave me an insight on why Charlie wasn't trying to fuck with me for real. Not only did Larisa let the cat out the bag, but since I was presumed dead on the street, these hoes wanted to let the world know they fucked in detail. Reading some of them had me shaking my head.

Rip Cheno. I'm going to miss all of our rendezvous. You were the best I ever had.

Damn Cheno. Why you had to leave me like this? God didn't make too many niggas who could touch my G-spot like you did. I hate that it ended like this. RIP

I can't believe you went out like this Cheno. You were supposed to left that bitch and made me your woman! I'm going to miss that dick you had between your legs. (Sorry to your girl), she should've sucked it better. According to these comments, I wasn't the only bitch getting fucked.

I closed the app in disgust because why air out what the hell you did with someone just to reveal the shit to rub in the face of the other person's partner. There were more women I was quite sure but I refused to continue reading to find out. Charlie was enough woman for me and I didn't have an excuse as to why I fucked around with other women. I knew exactly why I did it and the reason was because I could. Some women were desperate to deal with a nigga in hopes of making him leave who they were with, or thinking their pussy was enough to tie them down. The latter was a myth for me. There were too many women in the world to choose from. But Charlie was the one for I wanted for the long haul.

There were light taps on the door then it opened. A food worker followed by a nurse entered the room. When the tray was placed in front of me, I lifted the lid and frowned. The chicken looked like it was a week old and the fries were cold. I closed that shit and grilled the worker.

"Take this back wherever you got it from. I wouldn't feed that shit to my dog if I had one."

The nurse lifted the lid and cringe. "Please take this back and have his food cooked fresh."

"No, that's aight. I don't want nothing from that kitchen."

The worker left with the food on the cart saying something in Spanish. If the remote wasn't attached to the bed, I would've hit her ass in the back of her head with it. My stomach growled loudly pissing me off even more.

"Mr. Brown, I'm about to go on lunch. You don't have any restrictions in your chart so I can bring you something back. What would you like?"

"Would it be out of your way to go get some jerk chicken?" I asked.

"Not at all. What would you like?"

"A white jerk chicken dinner with cabbage, greens, candied yams, macaroni and cheese, and rice and beans. Make sure they put extra hot jerk sauce in the bag. Do you have Cashapp or Apple Pay?"

"You don't need to send money. I'll cover it." Cutting my eyes at her, she got the hint. "I have both but you can send it to my Apple Pay." The nurse gave me her number and I sent the money to her. When she got the notification, she took out her phone and gasped. "That's too much money."

"No, it's enough to cover the food for both of us and gas money for your whip. We all good."

I watched as she did something on her phone and took in her features. Baby girl was thick. A chocolate beauty with short hair, a big ass, with a pretty smile to match. The hoe in me was activated and I couldn't keep my thoughts to myself. My inner self was telling me not to go there, but I went against the grain.

"What's your name, Shawty?"

"It damn sure ain't Shawty." She paused to look at me. "It's Amari."

"A pretty name for a beautiful woman. So, Miss Amari, where's your man?"

"Where's your woman today? She wouldn't allow anyone to do their job taking care of your hygiene. That was an indication that you were a taken man. Am I wrong, Mr. Brown?"

I laughed lowly because Charlie left me then wanted to cockblock while I was in a coma. To just turn around and reiterate the fact that we weren't together. She was wild.

"That was my ex. We broke up right before I was shot. So, to answer your question, no, I'm not taken by anyone. Your turn." I smirked.

"I'm single as well. For the record, drama is something I don't want to be involved in. As you can see, I'm a nurse and majority of the time I'm married to my career. It's what's important to me at this time."

"You saying all that like you don't allow yourself to have friends."

"We can talk more when I come back. I placed the order on the website and it should be ready by the time I get there."

"Do yo' thang. Where am I going?"

Amari put her phone in the pocket of her scrub and left the room. I watched the way her cheeks clapped with every step she took. As I added her name to her number, I made plans to keep in touch with her. My phone rang and a number I didn't recognize was on the display. Almost declining the call, I remembered the call from G I was waiting on.

"Yo. Who this?"

"Aye, this is Grant Davenport. I'm looking for Cheno."

"What's up, G. Thanks for calling. I was expecting yo' call."

"Good. Look, I don't think talking over the phone is the best thing to do. Pearl said you will be released tomorrow."

"That's right. You can come out to my crib and we can chop it up there."

"Sounds like a plan. You straight though, right?"

"Yeah, I'm good. I just have to wear a cast on my arm and the gunshot wounds will heal in time. I'll take it."

"I feel you. Look, tell yo' sister to put out the word that your memorial will take place the day after tomorrow."

"My memorial?"

"Yeah, nigga. You can't just make these muthafuckas think you're dead without having a service," G explained. "I have a homie who has a funeral home we can use."

"Hol' up! It's one thing to accept the fact that I'm supposed to be dead, but y'all taking that shit to another level if you expect me to act the shit out. Who you think about to get in a casket to test out its comfortableness? Not me! Man, you crazy."

I was on the verge of hanging up on that nigga. This wasn't no motion fuckin' picture. I didn't play those type of games. G was gon' have to come better than that because I didn't want no parts of that shit. The seriousness was all in my tone and this nigga was laughing as if I told a joke. I didn't see nothing funny about the circumstances.

"I'm sorry for laughing but you have to be strategic when it comes to things of this nature, Cheno. There has to be proof their mission was accomplished. I'm not asking you to get casket sharp. As a matter of fact, you won't even be in the building. The plan is, you were cremated. There will be no body. Just an empty urn sitting in the front of the room with your family and friends talking about yo' ass," G said with a hint of humor still in his tone.

"Oh, I can go with that. Playing with the dead is definitely not my forte. Muthafucka end up getting fitted for a box for real," I said shaking my head.

"Aight. Lock me in." he laughed. "Go take a shit because I know you need to. Hit me when you get to the crib."

"No doubt."

Once again, I saved the number in my phone and contemplated calling Charlie. She would've been the first person I called to tell her about some shit like that. But I had to remember her ass wasn't talking to me and was out *on a date*. Charlie better have all the fun she could to get her lick back. When I decided enough was enough, that shit was dead.

Chapter 12

Tank

"How the fuck you work for this nigga and don't know shit about what's going on over there, Sketty?"

I had to get on this muthafucka because he was digging in his ass with the information he was supposed to provide. Cheno's been dead for almost a week and there was no word on when his family was going to lay his punk ass to rest. Sketty came through when he told us Cheno suspected that nigga Free of being involved with his trap getting hit. He lured Free to his death. It was brilliant to make it seem as if he committed suicide. Open and close case for CPD.

We got Cheno out the way and one of his workers. Now it was time to eliminate everybody associated with him. I just needed to know who those people were. Honey was off limits because she was all Cheese talked about nowadays. He was playing with hot water in my opinion. I tried to explain to him that Honey wasn't stupid by far. She knew who was involved in Cheno's death, but all my cousin thought about was the love he had for her. I'd never wanted him to be with Letty until Cheese decided to get Honey back into his life. She was going to be the one to stop his heart from beating.

Nobody could tell me that Honey forgave Cheese for turning his back on her. Then to get out of prison to find out the man you loved is fucking around with your ex best friend. Ain't no way a female is going to forgive and be down with nigga that did her like that. Cheese was going to learn the hard way and I will be the one to say, I told you so.

"Every time I'm at the trap asking questions, nobody has an answer. It's like his family is keeping everything secret. To make matters worse, there's no money being kept at none of the spots no more. I don't know what's going on."

I grilled this muthafucka trying to see if there was some indication that he was on that Tina Snow. His ass had to be on something because a blind man could see that he was being kept out of the know of what was going on. This just validated what I already thought. Cheno's team was weak as fuck. And I had dumber sitting in my passenger seat.

"Nigga, they not telling you shit because they're on yo' ass! You never picked up on the vibes when you around them? I know there were signs. Them niggas probably followed yo' stupid ass a time or two when we met up."

"Nah, they not treating me different. There's no reason for anybody to follow me around," Sketty said with confidence.

"If I was in Cheno's people shoes, I'm doing my own investigation on everybody that's in my circle. According to you, and correct me if I'm wrong, didn't you tell me that Cheno had no beef with anybody?"

"Yeah, I said that."

"Then all of a sudden, his trap gets hit. He thought it was Free, but couldn't question him because he was already unknowingly dead, right?" Sketty nodded. "Okay, then Cheno gets hit soon after and they don't know shit. Yeah, okay. Your head is on the chopping block and you don't even know it. You are a suspect now."

I took out a blunt because I had the urge to smoke. After a couple of tokes, I went in on his ass again.

"I'm gon' give my take on this. It's been quiet because they're plotting. You need to tell me who is somebody Cheno loved and his people will do whatever to protect?"

It was time for me to make some shit happen because waiting on Sketty to get what I needed was a waste of time. He could be cool with playing the wait game, but me on the other hand knew nothing good could come from doing that. Honey was probably going to be the one I snatched up with or without Cheese's approval.

"His sister. Cheno always had us looking out for her when he wasn't around," Sketty finally spoke. "She isn't your average female though. Breeze can handle herself like the best of them."

"That's a start. Where can I find her?"

"Cheno never disclosed where they lived. Honey has a mechanic shop 111th and Stewart. Breeze works there. She also sells weed on the side and be over there on 59th and Loomis."

I mentally stored the information in my memory then turned the key in the ignition. "Be ready when I hit yo' line. We gon' get at his sis and get the ball going. I think we should pay her a visit at the shop. Catch her ass slipping. I'm gon' go find her on social media and learn a little bit about the bitch."

"I'm friends with her. Hold on," Sketty said scrolling through his phone. "She just made a post thirty minutes ago. It says...

*As y'all know, my brother **Cheno** was murdered. I wasn't ignoring anyone that was calling to give condolences, I just wasn't in the head space to continuously talk about losing Cheno. For y'all you bitches posting on his page letting it be known you fucked, keep that shit a buck and tell the whole truth. Cheno didn't love you hoes. He may have hit, but I bet that's all he did. Keep my brother's name out ya mouth.*

For those who truly gave a damn about my brother. His services will be eleven o'clock Friday morning at Dyson Funeral Home. 3240 W, 79th Street. Do not come with the bullshit. You will get yo' shit rocked. On my mama.

"Bingo! That's where we're going to make shit happen. Send me the link to her page so I can check her out. I'm about to get out of here. I'll holla at you in a minute. Make sure you're at that funeral. If you don't go, it would look suspicious as hell."

"I'll be there. Just let me know the plan so I will know how to react."

"I got you."

I left Sketty's slow ass on the curb and didn't wait for him to get back to his car. I went to my mom's house to check on her then went straight home. I tried calling Cheese but he didn't answer but I knew he would hit me back in due time. I sat on my couch with a bottle of Dussè and a blunt as I scrolled Cheno sister's social media. She really didn't post on much giving me nothing to go on. I won't lie though, baby girl had skills with the car wraps. Too bad it wouldn't be long that she'd enjoy her craft.

I was thinking about who I could send to the funeral home to wreak havoc. One person came to mind. Going to the contact, I waiting as the phone rang.

"What up, Tank."

"Aye, I got a job for you. Would you be available Friday morning?"

"Give me more information. I'm not busy but I need to know what's up."

"Cheno's family is having his funeral and I need you there to air that bitch out. I need a fresh face. If I could do it myself, I would."

"Hell yeah! I haven't gotten my hands dirty in quite some time. My personal get back will come in due time. Until then, I don't have a problem dusting off my guns. Text me the location and time and I'm there."

"Good looking my nigga. I'm about to send that too you soon as I hang up."

"Aight, bet."

My dude has never let me down. Shit was about to get hectic and I was ready to strap up. I went downstairs to the basement of my house and opened the gun closet I had. The drugs and money I snatched from Cheno's trap was stacked in the back and the money was hidden in the safe in the floorboards. Rubbing my hands together like Birdman, I smiled from ear to ear as I took in the scene before me. It wasn't easy being a jack boy, but made that shit look like it was.

Taking an AR15 from the rack, I caressed that muthafucka like it was a bitch. I couldn't wait to use the hollow point bullets that were stored in a thirty-round drum. Somebody was going to look like Swiss cheese when I finished with them. It was going to be one of those niggas, I had other plans for Cheno's sister. My phone rang and it was Cheese.

"Cuz, where you at?" I said when the call connected.

"I'm at the crib with Letty. What's going on?"

"I got some news for you. Cheno's funeral is going to be Friday morning. I already called Dro to shake some shit up."

"Good shit. We both know we wouldn't be able to show our faces so that was a good decision. This is about to put things in motion so be ready so you don't have to get ready. I need your head a hundred percent in the game. Did you tell him that Honey is not to be touched?"

This nigga. I couldn't believe out of all the shit I said, he was still caught up on Honey. What we were about to do was going to stir shit up with everybody close to Cheno, including Honey. I had to try one more time to get him to see that pursuing something with her was the wrong thing to do at this time.

"Cheese, I think you need to stay away from Honey. You can't be that gullible to think she don't know by now that we're responsible for what happened. You telling me to have my head in the game and yours is in between Honey's legs mentally. I think you need to take heed to your own lecture, my nigga."

"Leave Honey to me. Just make sure Dro knows not to hurt her in any type of way. Letty is on her way back in here. I gotta go."

Cheese hung up fast and I swear that nigga rode the same short yellow bus as Sketty back in the day. I grabbed my AR, 9mm,.380, and plenty of ammo before I headed to my whip. It was time to go out into the middle of nowhere and shoot at some cans. Hell, I may shoot an animal or two for dinner. But what I wasn't going to do was sit idle trying to figure out how I was going to keep my cousin alive.

Chapter 13

Charlie

I was tired as hell as I dressed to head to the shop. Sleep didn't come easy once I did settle down for the night. My date with Caesar started out great until he pushed the gifts on me. To me it was like he didn't hear me when I told him I wasn't ready for anything serious. Most men didn't do things for a woman without looking for something in return and I wasn't the type to have a man assuming anything. Women of today would call me stupid for not taking the gifts but I didn't care about material things. What I wanted was priceless and that was for Caesar to get to know me on every level leading up to being with me.

The next man I decide to settle down with will be my best friend, as well as my lover. Hell, he had to be my Big Dawg when it was all said and done. Pulling my hair into a ponytail, I slipped my feet into my shoes. With keys in hand and my purse on my shoulder, I waltz through the house. When I opened the door, I was met with the shock of my life. Everything Caesar tried to give me last night was sitting on the porch.

There were bags from Pandora, Louis Vuitton, Tiffany's, Christian Louboutin, and the big bouquet of roses. When I took a closer look at the bouquet, there were hundred-dollar bills folded to replicate the shape of the roses. It had to be two or three hundred of them if I had to guess. I wasn't going to find out because I wasn't accepting any of it. Taking my phone from my purse, I called Caesar despite it being eight in the morning.

"Yeah," he answered groggily.

"Good morning, Caesar. Would you please come outside and get these gifts? There was a reason I left them at Brisco's with you last night."

"Charlie, the gifts are yours. Stop fighting what's bound to happen naturally." I could hear him shuffling around. "My intentions are not to buy you into being with me. I can have any woman out there but my desire is with you."

I was conflicted and didn't have anything to say in return. Caesar on the other hand kept speaking his mind.

"I don't know what dude did to you, but I'm not him. All that shit you said last night went in one ear and out the other." He paused as I listened to what sounded like him brushing his teeth.

"Just come get this stuff because I have to be at work soon."

The silence made me remove the device from my ear and sure enough, Caesar had hung up on my ass. I was about to storm over to his house when he emerged wearing a pair of basketball shorts and slides. His chest was bare. My mouth went cotton ball dry as I followed his every move with my eyes. Caesar was fine and he knew it. His strides were so precise that he appeared to move in slow motion. Before I knew it, his strong arms were wrapped around my waist and his lips were pressed against mine.

My kitty purred in delight because she hadn't been tampered with in months. But I had to disappoint her because nothing was happening. I broke the kiss and stepped back and diverted my eyes away from him.

"Um, take the gifts, Caesar. I need to go."

He smiled and bent down and grabbed all the bags in both of his hands and walked them inside of the house. I placed my hands on my hips in disbelief because I'd told him I didn't want the gifts. Caesar emerged and picked up the bouquet. When he walked back into the house, I followed. Didn't have time to play his games.

"Caesar——"

My voice was cut off as he once again covered my mouth with his. I didn't know when he placed the bouquet down but his hands cupped my face as he slipped his tongue into my mouth. My thong leaked and my legs weakened but he wrapped his arm around my waist to hold me up. *This can't happen!* I screamed in my head. The words never left my mouth. Caesars hand caressed my ample ass and my tunnel leaked.

I lost the battle to fight not having sex with him and found myself massaging his pipe through his shorts. Caesar moaned into my mouth and reached behind me. The sound of the door slamming caused me to flinch. He picked me up above his head and placed me against the wall. The way he held me with one arm and maneuvered my leggings over my hips, I was paralyzed in anticipation. With my yoni on full display, Caesar slightly lifted my legs so they were on his shoulders.

"Damn, she's beautiful," he said licking his lips.

Caesar dove in head first French kissing my lower lips. I grabbed the back of his head as he sucked all the nectar from my body. Trying to suppress the moan that was caught in my throat was an epic failure because I came hard and hell out seductively.

"Fuck!" I moaned grinning into his mouth.

"Mmmhmm."

He never lost the beat to whatever song was playing in his head. Caesar was eating me like he was on death row and I was his last meal request. My stomach clinched tightly as I rode his tongue. It was so stiff that I could've sworn it was a dick I was riding. The thickness of it satisfied me over and beyond with the combination of sucks and licks. Holding back was no longer an option. I moan, purred, clawed at his head, and tried to run, but there wasn't any escape from the tongue-lashing Caesar was dishing out.

"I'm cummin'! Oh my God!" I shrieked.

Caesar was enjoying every bit of his performance because he went harder. The friction on my pussy felt so good and a few seconds later, his face and chest were soaked with my juices. My legs shook uncontrollably and I couldn't stop the orgasm. Giving my lower lips a final smooch, Caesar lifted my legs over his head and placed me on my feet.

"Go cleanup and have a great day at work. I'll be waiting when you get off," he said kissing me quickly before leaving.

I was stuck for a few minutes then realized I needed to get to work. I duck walked all the way to the bathroom with a smile. Caesar's tongue was lethal and I could only imagine what his dick game was like. I took a quick shower and raced out of the house. Caesar and I didn't have sex but that's not the way I felt. His oral touch had me giddy and I wanted more. My phone rang and Taz's name appeared on the dash.

"On my way. I'm on the expressway and there's an accident."

"Okay, I'll be in my car."

I arrived ten minutes later and opened up the shop. Breeze walked in a few minutes later. Taz walked over kissing and hugging on her. They parted ways as Breeze's first client came in. She told him to pull his car around back then she headed toward the wrap room. When she passed my station, Breeze paused.

"There's something different about you. I can't put my finger on it," she said looking me over. "Yo' ass glowing. Let me find out you been fuckin'." She laughed.

"Not fuckin' but he did get a taste of the rainbow. Don't tell your brother."

Breeze scowled. "That's yo' business. What you do has nothing to do with me. If this man makes you happy, go for that shit. You and Cheno are no longer together, Charlie. I appreciate you being there while he was in a coma and looking out for him. Many women out here would've said fuck him after what he was doing behind their back. If anything, I commend you for still being loyal to his ass."

"Thank you, Breeze."

"No thanks needed. You have to do what's best for you. Dealing with a muthafucka constantly playing in your face only leads to your unhappiness. Depression looks good on no one. I'm just glad you were broken before knowing your worth. I have to tell you though. Cheno's been asking about the nigga you went on a date with. Don't tell me shit about him then I won't have to lie. If I don't know, I can't tell."

I nodded with understanding because Breeze always kept it real no matter if the truth would hurt. It didn't surprise me that Cheno was asking who I was with last night. I was the one who revealed I was on a date. He couldn't be mad because he did more than just went on dates when we were together. What I was doing wasn't called cheating. We weren't together. A woman came in for an oil change taking my mind off Cheno's probing but I could still feel Caesar's mouth on my yoni.

Working hard for three hours straight, I finally took a lunch break. I hadn't eaten breakfast and I was starving. Breeze walked into the breakroom as I looked through the menus to figure out what I wanted to eat.

"What you doing?" she asked sitting in the chair across from me.

"I'm trying to figure out what I want to eat."

"I ordered chicken from Harold's. Honey is going to pick it up on her on her way here."

"Thanks."

Sitting the menus to the side, my mind went back to the sexual tryst I endured hours prior. The feeling I had was one I hadn't had in months. Caesar had wakened up the freak in me. Breeze's voice interrupted my thoughts.

"I want you to know that we're having Cheno's memorial tomorrow."

Looking at her strangely, I didn't understand what she was talking about. "What do you mean? Cheno is alive, Breeze. He's alright."

"He is but those niggas still don't know that. We have to make it seem like they really did what they set out to do. This shit is far from over."

I held my head down then looked up with tears burning my eyes. "I can't see him lying in a casket. I'm not going."

"He won't be in a casket, Charlie. It's a memorial. We will have an empty urn sitting on a stand in the front of the funeral home. Cheno will be at home chilling until the shit is over. You have to be there, sis."

Wiping the tears away I felt better after she explained. Cheno may have done me wrong, but it didn't mean I hated him. If he had died, I would still be crushed beyond repair. The love I had for that man was still strong, I just knew we were better off apart. If it was meant to be, it will be. Until then, I was ready to live my life happy and free."

"How did the wrap turn out?"

"That shit was fye! My client loved it. The clientele I have is growing. Word of mouth is a muthafucka, not to mention my promotion of my work on social media. I hooked my hip up and that was supposed to be the end of that shit, but the man upstairs wasn't going to allow me to sleep on my craft."

"And I wasn't either! Let me see what you pimped out this time," Honey said coming in with a handful of chicken.

The aroma filled my nostrils and I stood to wash my hands. Taz walked in doing the same. When lunchtime came around, the sign automatically went on the front door. We always ate together no matter what. Heading to the table, Breeze order about thirty wings with white bread, fries, coleslaw, and mild sauce on the side. I wasted no time putting six wings on a plate with a pile of fries. They could keep the coleslaw because I would throw that shit in the garbage.

"Honey, why didn't you and Quell come back to the room yesterday? Was he mad about the plan?"

"Breeze, we left because he wanted to argue and I'm not with that shit," Honey said sitting down with her food. "I had to explain that he wasn't my man as if he didn't know this already. Fucking didn't mean we were a couple. Quell is against what I'm doing, but what can he do about it? Nothing."

"So, he's still mad?" Breeze asked eating a fry.

"If that's what you want to call it. Quell called himself punishing me. When I tell you the man pulled out all punches in the bedroom. He brought Velcro straps to my house and attached my hands to my ankles, bitch. That man ate my pussy 'til I cried and I couldn't do nothing but take that shit. Then, he handcuffed my arms and legs to the bed and fucked me like a porn star."

"Okay, that's enough. I'm eating." Breeze laughed.

"Fuck that, ask him where he got that shit from. I need that in my life!" I exclaimed.

"I'll ask him but it's gonna be a minute before Cheno can handle you like that."

"Who said anything about Cheno?" I smirked.

The room grew quiet because I hadn't talked to anyone outside of Breeze about being with someone else. They all knew what Cheno had done and how I felt about it so they shouldn't be surprised. Taz took a sip from her Sprite, Honey shook her head, and I continued to eat like it was nothing.

"I don't want to know. Cheno ain't about to be questioning me about who you're with. We gon' deal with this like the code of the streets, the less I know the better," Honey said. "Anyway, y'all ready for this damn memorial? Quell told me about it."

"I'm ready to get this shit over with to be honest. We have to keep our head on the swivel because I have a feeling them niggas gon' come through on bullshit," Breeze replied.

"Cheese still hasn't said anything about what happened to Cheno. I guess he thinks if he doesn't bring it up, I won't suspect him. He's wrong as fuck though." Honey laughed. "I was talking to him via Messenger last night. In his last voice message, I heard Letty asking who he was talking to in the background. He hasn't said shit else since. The nigga said he was going to leave her alone but I knew that was a lie. It's going to be hard for him to toggle two bitches and get away with it without his bitch finding out."

"She's in her feelings because she stays on social media talking about niggas ain't shit, and if you want me to be this, a nigga gotta do that type of shit. She's too loud for no damn reason."

"Yeah, it sounds like she's doing too much. The bitch gon' go into cardiac arrest when she finds out it's you." I cut in.

We all dug into our food and all that could be heard was the smacking of our lips. I looked at my Apple watch and noticed the time flew past. We would have to get back to work soon.

"I got a twelve o'clock appointment so I gotta go smoke."

Breeze got up and went out the back door. I took a few more bites finishing off my chicken then started cleaning up. Taz had already walked back up front and Honey left toward the office. Covering the remaining chicken, I made my way to the refrigerator and opened the door. A slew of gunshots had me dropping what was in my hands fleeing to the backdoor. Breeze was on her back pulling the trigger to her Nina. There was no need for me to help because the perpetrator was already lying flat on his back bleeding out.

"Call the cleanup crew and tell them to hurry up," she said getting to her feet.

Doing as she asked, I made the call and followed her down the walkway. Honey and Taz rounded the corner and stopped in their tracks. I rushed to where they stood.

"Go back to the front and lock the door. I have to close the gate so nobody walks up on this shit before the crew gets here."

Without hesitation, I pulled the gates closed and secured the locks. It was Cheno's idea to install the gates for us to park our cars, but we never used it until that moment. There wasn't an exit point on the other end and that was a blessing for us. The last thing we needed was the police coming through and there was a dead body lying on the ground.

"This muthafucka." Breeze huffed. "Yeah, you came for the wrong one, nigga. Now rot in hell you snake ass bitch!"

I went to see who the fuck would come shooting and looked down. Low and behold it was Sketty lying face up with his eyes open and his gun lying next to his hand. Breeze shot him with all chest shots. Somebody was looking out for her because she wasn't shot once.

"Cheno not gon' believe this shit," she said taking out her phone.

Chapter 14

Quell

I was in my shop setting up equipment when I heard gunshots. My first thought was Honey. Me and my homies Foot, Wolf, and Stubs ran out of the tattoo shop and down the pavement. When I got to the door, it was locked. Taking out my phone, I called her up and she answered on the first ring.

"Open the door," I said calmly.

It took a few minutes for Honey to open the door and that scared the fuck out of me. When she finally did, she stepped back and allowed us to enter. I expected her to be shook, but that wasn't the vibe I picked up. Honey was pissed. She turned her back and began to walk away. Grabbing her arm, I looked down at her.

"What happened? I heard the shots."

"Sketty tried to take Breeze out. He was too slow and is now lying out back with his chest open. This is why I have to do what I'm doing with Cheese. The nigga doesn't want to do his own dirty work." She gritted. "But he's going to wish he had."

"Did y'all call Cheno?" Soon as the words left my mouth, my phone rang. "I'm already here."

"Tell Honey to close up for the day." Cheno barked.

I put the phone on speaker. "Say that again. She can hear you."

"Honey, I need you to close the shop for the day. Ain't no telling what them niggas plan to do next."

"I'm not missing out on money——"

"Fuck that money!" Cheno yelled cutting her off. "Y'all lives are in jeopardy and you talking about money! Be fuckin' for real, Honey. Close that muthafucka down and reschedule your clients 'til Monday. I'll pay you for the four days."

Instead of responding, Honey walked off. There was a new side to her that I hadn't seen since meeting her and that was probably one of the reasons she didn't want to commit to a relationship. The fire in her eyes were deadly and I never wanted to be on the other end of the target.

"Cheno, I'll make sure she closes the shop. What do you need me to do?"

"I just got a call from Breeze. The cleanup crew is there. Make sure there's no trace of that nigga. I should've listened to Fredo when he told me there was something off about that nigga Sketty. You live and you learn though. Let me know when y'all get out of there."

"Bet."

Retracting the path Honey took, me and the homies found our way to the back of the shop. There was a black van backed into the walkway and not a body in sight. One of the crew members were power washing the pavement and it didn't look like someone had been shot at all. They were good at their job and that's what I loved to see. Thorough niggas taking care of business. Honey came over to me with a smug look.

"I've rescheduled all of the appointments. Relay the message to your boy. I'm out."

"Go straight home, Honey and call me when you get there."

"Okay," she said walking away.

"Follow her and make sure she good," I said to Foot.

He made a beeline to the lot as I watched as her get in the car. Honey was in my line of sight until her whip exited the parking lot and blended into traffic with Foot right behind her.

"Aye Breeze, you good?" I asked.

"Yeah, bro. Pussy ass niggas thought they would catch me slipping. The joke's on them now. One mo' down and I don't know how many mo' to go. I'm ready though. Why these muthafuckas coming for me is the question that has me fucked up. They already got Cheno; so they think. What do I have that brought them my way?"

"I don't know because whatever it is, they wouldn't have gotten whatever it was because you would've been dead. Dead folks don't talk. That's something I have to bring to Cheno's attention. It could also be to eliminate anybody associated with him all together."

"It don't even matter because it's up from here," Breeze said observing the crew over her shoulder. "Y'all finished? I need to get away from here."

"Yeah. We about to make this lil problem disappear for good. Be careful out here, sis."

"At all times," she said in return.

The van pulled out like they had just cut the grass or some shit. I waited for Breeze to lock up the shop and made sure she along with Charlie, and Taz got in their vehicles before I walked back to my spot. Wolf locked the door and I went back to setting up equipment. I was hoping to open up soon and needed everything in place. The delivery for Ink beds, armrests, equipment stands, and UV sanitizers. I'll be doing interviews for artists once this shit with Cheno is laid to rest.

"Aye, Quell, tell me what's going on with these niggas again. Cause I don't understand how females are the target now that Cheno is dead to them."

"I don't know what they got going on, but Cheno better end this shit once and for all. If something happens to Honey, I'm gon' have to whoop his ass."

"It's not gon' come to that. We gon' silence these soft niggas easily. If Cheno's sister can handle them like she did dude today, they ain't on shit."

We laughed at that because he wasn't wrong. My phone rang and it was Foot. He told me Honey was safe inside her home. I advised him to stay at my crib until I got there. Foot knew what to do and he would know if Honey was leaving. I'd installed cameras outside my crib and one was facing the front of hers.

Me, Wolf, and Stubs worked hard for a few more hours at the shop. After closing up, we jumped in my truck and I made the drive to Cheno's crib. When I pulled up, there were three cars in the driveway. We hopped out and walked up the driveway. The door opened and Fredo stood waiting for us.

"What's up, fam?" I asked giving him a brotherly hug.

"Shit. Just trying to figure out how we gon' go after these niggas. Sis handled her business, huh?"

"I didn't get a chance to see the damage because the cleanup crew were on their job."

Walking deeper into the house, I found Cheno sitting on the couch with two other niggas. With all the shit going on, everybody was being looked at under a microscope. I didn't trust nobody I didn't know shit about. Security alert was high at that point.

"Aye, Cheno, who these muthafuckas?" I asked. Before he could answer one of them stood to his feet mugging the fuck out of me. If he thought I was going to back down, he was sadly mistaken.

"I can tell you're not from around here because your accent screams Georgia. I know you looking out for ya boy and I respect that, but don't bring that street shit in here like you about to air this bitch out. We not against y'all, we here to help y'all clean up this shit."

Wolf and Stubs walked up and stood next to me ready for whatever. That only made his ass grill us harder. Cheno knew how the fuck we got down and he too stood to his feet before anything could go down.

"Scony, nah, we not even about to do that. Sit down bro." The other unfamiliar dude said rising up from his seat.

"Quell, it's cool, my nigga." Cheno said. "These are my people. They straight."

Scony shook his head and sat on the barstool at the island. I stood with my arms folded over my chest waiting for him to say something else to me. even though Cheno said they were cool, like I said, I didn't trust no muthafuckin' body at that point.

"Aye, we not here to fight each other. We are now a team of muthafuckas that is trying to come up with a plan to put all the bullshit that's going on to an end. Trying to figure out who has the biggest dick isn't part of the plan. Save that anger for the niggas in the streets. We need a game plan and we not leaving this muthafucka 'til we got one in place." He looked over at Scony and the nigga nodded in agreement.

"I'm G," he said walking up to me with his hand held out. I looked at his ass for a second before shaking him up. "We not the enemies, youngblood. One thing about the streets, you need to learn not to approach an unknown situation with aggressiveness. That shit can get you killed because niggas nowadays shoot first and ask questions after the fact. Then it's too late because yo' ass will be dead. Think smart, homie. Have a seat so we can get this shit in order and go about our day."

Wolf walked toward a chair across from where Cheno was siting. "What up, fam."

"What's good? I didn't know you were coming. Where's Foot?"

"Yeah, Quell told me what was up and I didn't hesitate to come through. You know I'm a phone call away if you need me to put in work." Cheno nodded. "Foot ass on Paw Patrol at Quell's crib."

"Watch that shit, nigga." I said causing everybody except Scony to laugh. "This my dude Stubs."

Cheno dapped him up and he too found a seat. The tension was leaving the room slowly as we made small talk. G cleared his throat. I decided to take a seat so I could pay close attention to the conversation that was about to be underway.

"Cheno, all of this started due to Tank hitting a lick off your trap, and one of your own helped him, right?"

"Yeah." Cheno agreed.

"How the fuck did it get this far?"

"G, none of that is going to end this shit. All we need to know is who's involved. So far, I know about Tank and Cheese. Who else?"

"Scony, we not trying to tear the city up."

"Yes, the fuck we are!" Cheno shouted. "Them muthafuckas went after my sister and all bets are off. After the memorial, I don't give a damn how much pain I'm in, I'll be out in the streets lighting up every block I know of until I find them niggas. As a matter of fact, I'm gon' start at Tank's mama's house."

G and the other nigga smiled when Cheno finished his rant. I was confused because G was just talking like a political ass Wall Street employee a minute ago. Whatever they were talking about before I arrived went out the window.

"That's the grit I was waiting on. It don't matter what condition you in long as you can walk, you can tackle the muthafucka who is trying to take you down. We gon' play this shit by ear and wait to see what goes down at the memorial."

"Fuck that," Scony said snatching a piece of paper and a pen from the coffee table. "I want every name that works for you. And I mean all your businesses. I'll have my nigga Quan to run the names. Starting with these three. Spit out those gov'ments. Now!"

We were at Cheno's house for damn near three hours listening to G, Scony, and Miss Pearl bark out orders. The way they were going through folks with a fine-tooth comb, there was no way Cheese and his crew was getting away with what they did. The bitch that set Cheno up better move like a thief in the night because they were on her ass and she didn't even know it. I pulled up to my crib but didn't go inside.

"What you sitting here for?" Stubs asked.

"I'm going over to Honey's. Y'all have a good night." I picked my phone up from the cupholder and sent Honey a text.

Unlock the door.

Getting out of the car, I jogged up the steps and turned the knob. It opened with ease and I entered. Honey was sitting on the couch with her finger to her mouth telling me to be quiet. She had the phone in her lap and I knew right away she was talking to that nigga Cheese.

"So, you gon' let me take you out tomorrow?"

"Cheese, I'm quite sure you heard by now that Cheno was killed. We're having his memorial tomorrow. I need to be with my family."

"I haven't really been out like that to be in the know. Last thing I heard was that Cheno got shot. It comes as a surprise to know he died."

My blood was boiling listening to this nigga lie through his teeth. He knew all about what happened because he orchestrated the shit.

"Look, I'm going to apologize for what Tank did when he stole from Cheno. I already said this shit to Cheno and he squashed that shit."

"That has nothing to do with me. I just hope the police finds the woman that shot my cousin. There was a witness and they are looking for her. It's going to take some time because all they have is a partial still photo."

"Damn, a bitch set him up?" Cheese asked.

"Yeah. We got her number out his phone but it's no longer in service. There's nothing the police can do with that. So, they say."

"I'm going to be here for you, Honey."

"How is that possible when you are still with my "best friend"?" Honey laughed. "I told you to get rid of Letty then we can talk about that."

"I'm not with Letty no more. She already moved back with her sister. If she was here, I wouldn't be on the phone with you."

"That don't mean nothing, Cheese. I'll take your word on it though. I have to get ready for tomorrow. I'll call if I need a shoulder to lean on."

"Do that. Honey, I swear I still love you even if you don't love me in return."

"I gotta go. Talk to you later." Honey ended the call and a tear fell from her face. "Did you hear how he lied without remorse? Cheese still thinks I'm the same gullible girl he used to deal with. And to say Cheno said fuck that his sticky-fingered ass cousin stole over two hundred thousand dollars from here is a crock of shit! My cousin ain't said nothing like that."

"Come on so I can run you a nice bath. We have a long day ahead of us tomorrow."

We walked into her room and I went into the bathroom to start her bath. Adding lavender scented bubble bath to the water, I went back into the bedroom. Honey was sitting where I left her with tears streaming down her face. Instead of asking what was wrong, I just hugged her tightly allowing her to weep. When her cries turned to sniffles, I lifted her into my arms and carried her into the bathroom. Undressing her, I held Honey's hand until she was resting comfortably.

"Would you please get my bath pillow from the linen closet? Right there in that door," she said pointing.

Getting the pillow for her, I placed it behind her head. Honey was so beautiful even when she was under a lot of stress. She closed her eyes and within minutes, she was sleeping like a baby. I lathered up a loofah and began washing her body. Not wanting to wake her just yet, I started massaging her scalp.

"That feels good. Thank you."

"You don't have to thank me. I'm supposed to make you feel good and not just sexually. Stand up so I can finish washing your body."

"Quell, I can bathe myself. Go into the bedroom and wait for me. I want you to be ready to give me a full body massage. I need it."

"And I got you." I winked with a smile before walking out the bathroom shutting the door behind me.

I took my clothes off and went into the other bathroom to shower. Honey had been out of prison two and a half months without truly enjoying herself in the process. It was my job to make sure she was stress free from this day forward. After washing thoroughly, I stepped out and dried my body then wrapped a towel around my waist. Entering the bedroom, Honey was lying flat on her stomach with her legs slightly opened. My mouth watered thinking about running my tongue along her slippery folds. But it wasn't about that, I wanted to make her cum with my touch. And I planned to do just that.

Chapter 15

Honey
"Baby, wake up."
I could feel the small kisses that Quell planted all over my face and neck. The last thing I wanted to do was get up and leave his arms. So instead of reacting, I pretended to still be sleeping and savored the affection I was receiving. The truth of the matter was Cheno's fake memorial was set to start at eleven and I really didn't want to attend. Something in the pit of my stomach told me it was going to be all bad.

"Honey, we have to get ready for the memorial," Quell whispered in my ear.

Turning over to face him, I palmed his face and I pulled him in for a kiss. It was the first time I'd initiated anything between us. After the massage he gave me last night, Quell did something Cheese could never do. Make love to my mind, body, and soul. I felt refreshed and rejuvenated.

"You kissing a nigga with dragon breath. Does that mean I'm in there?" Quell asked playfully nudging the side of my face with his nose.

"Some' like that. Thank you for the massage. I didn't realize how much I needed it. I slept like a baby."

"Yeah, I know. Slobbing and all. You almost turned this bed into a waterbed." He laughed. "I wanted to make you a bib but your head was too heavy on my arm and I couldn't move."

"You lying!"

"No, I'm not. Next time I'm gon' record yo' wet mouth ass. Anyway, get up and get ready."

I sat up on the side of the bed staring at the floor. The feeling in my stomach came back instantly. Something was going to happen at the memorial or sometime that day. The feeling was intense and I could no longer keep it to myself.

"Quell, I don't want to go to the memorial. I have a bad feeling about this. We should call it off."

"That can't happen. I promise you will be safe. We have plenty of people who will be in place to make sure that happens. We're only going to play this shit out as if Cheno is really dead. No more than an hour tops. There won't be a viewing or none of that shit. It's to give people the opportunity to say their goodbyes without a body."

I got up and went into the bathroom to freshen up. Flat ironing my hair after getting out of the shower, I applied a light coat of makeup and went back into the bedroom. Quell had already laid the Prada pantsuit I planned to wear on the bed. He was nowhere in sight and I figured he was in the other bathroom getting himself together. My phone rang and I rushed to answer it. Quell's picture was on display.

"Where are you?" I asked.

"I went home to get dressed. I knew you would think I was still in the house and didn't want to alarm you. I'll be outside in thirty minutes waiting in the car."

"Okay."

Quell hung up and I took my time dressing. Before I put the suit jacket over my black silk cami, I walked into the closet and fished the gun holster from the top shelf. When I have it in place, I take my 9mm from the lockbox and inserted it inside. I added another fully loaded clip, then I threw my jacket over it. There was no way I was going out feeling the way I was without protection. As I searched my closet for a pair of shoes, right away I bypassed the heels. Instead, I chose a pair of black flats that were comfortable on my feet.

Swapping out purses, I put my phone, wallet and .22 caliber pistol in my small black and silver Louis Vuitton. As I attached my silver band Apple watch on my wrist, I noticed I was five minutes past the time Quell said he would be outside. Walking swiftly to the door I opened it and stepped onto the porch. As he stated, Quell was standing outside his truck as his guys were parked behind and in front of him. Locking up, I walked slowly toward Quell.

Once we were inside the truck, we took off. Music was playing low on the stereo system but I wasn't paying attention to what it was. My focus was on what we were up against at the service. Quell grabbed my hand and kissed the back of it. I smiled on the inside but it never made it to my face. He did that several times until we pulled into the parking lot of the funeral home. It was packed with cars. Scanning the lot, it was going to be impossible to spot anyone that was against us.

Cheno's crew were scattered around standing guard. There were quite a few other guys as well and I knew they were there for us because they all had blue handkerchiefs tucked inside the left pocket of their jackets. Quell parked next to Breeze's Camaro and I reached for the door.

"I got that. Sit tight," he said getting out to open the door for me. "I want you to stay by my side at all times. Or at least in my eyesight."

"Okay," I said before he kissed me tenderly.

We walked inside and Breeze stood in the doorway behind a lady who was handing out obituaries. Seeing Cheno's picture on the front brought tears to my eyes. Knowing nothing about the events that were real didn't stop me from thinking about the what if it was and that's what bothered me the most. Cheno being shot could've easily landed him in this very funeral home in reality.

"Good act, cuz." Breeze whispered as she hugged me tightly.

"These tears are real. Watch yourself, Breeze, some shit is going to go down here."

"I'm strapped and so are many others. We're ready for whatever, are you?"

"You know I am. Double time."

Stepping back, Breeze turned towards the room where the service was set to take place. There were more women than men in attendance. Cheno was lucky he didn't have any kids running around all over the city. He may be somebody's daddy and just didn't know about it.

"I hope these hoes keep their mouths closed today." Breeze mumbled. "Did you see all that shit on Cheno's page?"

"No, what happened?"

"Bitches shouted loud for the world to know how they busted it open for Cheno's hoe ass. The shit was funny too because that's when the arguments started. Goofass hoes going back and forth about who he was fuckin' with. It was embarrassing as hell."

My cousin had these females' wilding out over him. I wanted to be a rat on the block when they found out he was very much alive. He was never going to fuck with them hoes again because one thing he hated was somebody telling his business. Especially on social media. There was no way to clear up what they'd said to attach themselves to his name.

The director came over informing us they were ready to start. At that moment, Charlie entered wearing a black dress, heels, and a hug black hat with a veil. I almost laughed because she was playing the hell out of the grieving girlfriend role. Her shades covered half her face. Quell walked in along with two guys I had never seen before. He stood in front of me clasping both of my hands in his.

"They're ready for us to be seated."

"Okay, in a minute. I want to introduce you to Grant Davenport and Demarius Jones. They're friends of Cheno."

"Nice to meet both of you." I smiled shaking their hands. "Are you by chance thee G and Scony from the Goon Squad?"

"Yeah, that's us. How did you know that?" G asked.

"My mama used to babysit Malikhi for his mother Lovely. I learned about his death while I was in prison. How's Lovely doing?"

"What's yo' mama's name?" Scony questioned.

"Victoria."

"Victoria Love? The bitch that live on 81st and Eberhart? The Victoria Love that was fuckin' with that nigga named James. Didn't his ass get killed?" I nodded. "Good for his pedophile ass. Lovely used to leave my nephew with anybody I see. Unfortunately, she died of an overdose not too long after Malikhi passed away. It's good to meet you, Shawty. They're ushering people inside. I think we should join them," Scony said turning to walk away.

"Likewise. I have one more question." I called out before he could get to far. "So my mama still live in the same place?"

"Yeah. It's a damn shame she hasn't reached out to inform you of that herself." Scony shook his head leaving me standing there thinking about paying my mama a visit.

The line was out the door and I was antsy as hell because the feeling in my stomach was back. I glanced around nervously causing Quell to squeeze my hand. We walked past all the people scattered about and made our way to the front. Breeze was whispering to Charlie, her facial expression was stern like a mother scolding a child. I sat next to her hearing the end of what was being said.

"Fuck these bitches! Fix yo' muthafuckin' crown and show them you ain't bothered. It's not a secret that Cheno had you out here looking like Bozo. What the fuck you mad for? After today, you go your way, and let him go his. Leave the bullshit for him to worry about."

I focused on the blue and black urn that sat on top of a podium in the center of the room with Cheno's name on it. The tears fell again as I laid my head on Quell's shoulder. The Pastor cleared his throat then said good morning. He began talking about Cheno and all he'd accomplished in life. He said the typical shit that was said after someone passed away but most of the people knew the truth. I didn't want to hear that shit because I knew my cousin was home chilling. Taking my airpods from my purse, I put one in my left ear and closed my eyes.

"What are you doing?" Quell asked.

"Tuning this shit out. I can't listen to this."

"Gone Forever" by Mary J Blige ft. Remy Ma took me to another place. With my eyes closed I hoped people who were watching thought I was grieving. Remy's verse almost made me start rapping along with her. I contained myself and rapped in my head loud and clear for my enjoyment.

You did me wrong
When a good girl gone, she gone forever
When a real bitch leave, you gone wish you never met her
And I'm a real bitch, don't make 'em like me no more
Before I share my bed, I'll sleep on floors
I told you, I'm a wife I can't be your whore
We different prices, I don't go for what she go for
Please keep your keys, I'm changing all these locks
Bout to find a real nigga and give him all this box
Tryna bring me down, I'll give him all this top
See, I got money boo
I do what I wanna do
And I've been a hundred proof
You turned me to a dog, I'm barking, woof
Now I'm gone, nigga, poof

I was so engulfed in the words Remy was saying I had it on repeat. I noticed people were lining up against the wall. Pausing the music, I paid attention to what was going on around me. Breeze stood and climbed the few steps onto the stage. Breathing heavily into the mic while glancing around the room, she faked a smile.

"Whew, I never thought I'd be doing this for my best friend, When Cheno took over the role of daddy slash big brother, he became a superhero in my world. The night our mother passed Cheno looked me in the face and said, Breeze, it's you and me, my nigga. We all we got. With my brother gone, who got me?"

Breeze held her head down shaking her head. I got up along with the rest of our crew rushing to her side. We encircled her into a group hug and shared a moment while the onlookers clapped.

"You got us, baby," Taz said for all of us.

"Thanks. I love y'all. I gotta get back to this shit." She chuckled. We stayed right there to support her.

"Sorry about that. This is hard for a thug." Laughs filled the room changing the mood a bit. "I want to thank all of you for coming out to celebrate my brother. It's greatly appreciated." Breeze paused. "The last thing I want to do is get into an altercation with anybody here. So, I'm going to say this nice as I can. There is a two-minute timer for anyone who wants to speak. We don't care who Cheno was sleeping with. If you're in the line to expose whatever relationship you had with him, you may sit down now. Whoever does anything of the sort will get their shit rocked. You've been warned."

"She sounds just like Cheno." Somebody laughed.

"The spectacle y'all put on via his social media page was ridiculous. Keep it there."

Breeze concluded what she wanted to say handing the mic to the first person. The line was long before my cousin took the stage, and there was only seven remaining when she was done. As promised, Breeze was close by in case one of them said the wrong shit. Everything went smoothly. After the eulogy, the service ended twenty minutes later. The funeral home emptied rather quickly and only family and friends were left inside.

"Where's Dawson?" Breeze asked one of her aunts.

"He said he would be here. I don't know what happened."

"That man will never do right when it comes to his first-born kids. Dawson only wants the payout. I don't want to hear nothing when I end up hurting y'all brother. Tell him to stay the fuck away from me. Respectfully."

Breeze left the room with the urn in hand and I was right behind her. As we exited the building, the guys were making sure everyone got to their cars safely. I was relieved that the service was drama free. All morning, I was expecting something bad to take place and that wasn't the case at all. I looked around for Charlie and she was nowhere in sight. I sped walked to Breeze's car before she could get inside.

"Hey, did Charlie leave?" I asked.

"Yeah, she's in her feelings about all the bitches that showed up for Cheno. Charlie got to let that shit go." Breeze looked over her shoulder and frowned. "Who the fuck is that nigga?"

I turned to see who she was talking about. A dark-skinned nigga wearing a black button up shirt, black dress pants, and his hands behind his back moving slowly in the direction of Quell. His focus wasn't on him, but there was something sinister in his eyes. Breeze and I reached behind our backs at the same time and took aim just as he revealed his hand. Scony reacted first giving the guys time to take cover. I aimed taking the first shot never taking my finger off the trigger. Breeze was busting like Cleo and it was enough to make that nigga stop shooting and run off.

Running the short distance to Quell, my heart fell to my ass. He was on the ground and his leg was bleeding. G was leaning against the building holding his arm, and Scony wasn't hit at all. I took off my jacket and tied it around Quell's leg to control the bleeding.

"Who the fuck was that?" I asked no one in particular.

"I got a small glimpse of his face. I don't know, but the nigga looks all too familiar. In fact, he resembles that nigga Kelvin," Scony said looking at G.

"It can't be." G grimaced. "We healed that wound."

"Sometimes, old scars don't heal. Now this shit got a lot to do with us," Scony said pulling his phone out. "Quan, give me everything you know on Kelvin Banks. Including family members. I need it ASAP!"

To Be Continued...

To catch up on Grant Davenport (G) and Demarius Jones (Scony), read A Distinguished Thug Stole My Heart.

FOLLOW ME:

Facebook Author Page:
https://www.facebook.com/MzMeesh

Facebook:
https://www.facebook.com/mesha.king1

Instagram:
https://www.instagram.com/author_meesha/

Twitter:
https://twitter.com/AuthorMeesha

TikTok:
https://vm.tiktok.com/TTPdkx6LEW/

Website:
www.authormeesha.com

Lock Down Publications and Ca$h Presents
Assisted Publishing Packages

BASIC PACKAGE	UPGRADED PACKAGE
$499	$800
Editing	Typing
Cover Design	Editing
Formatting	Cover Design
	Formatting
ADVANCE PACKAGE	**LDP SUPREME PACKAGE**
$1,200	$1,500
Typing	Typing
Editing	Editing
Cover Design	Cover Design
Formatting	Formatting
Copyright registration	Copyright registration
Proofreading	Proofreading
Upload book to Amazon	Set up Amazon account
	Upload book to Amazon
	Advertise on LDP, Amazon and
	Facebook Page

***Other services available upon request.
Additional charges may apply

Lock Down Publications
P.O. Box 944
Stockbridge, GA 30281-9998
Phone: 470 303-9761

Submission Guideline

Submit the first three chapters of your completed manuscript to ldpsubmissions@gmail.com. In the subject line add **Your Book's Title**. The manuscript must be in a Word Doc file and sent as an attachment. Document should be in Times New Roman, double spaced, and in size 12 font. Also, provide your synopsis and full contact information. If sending multiple submissions, they must each be in a separate email.

Have a story but no way to send it electronically? You can still submit to LDP/Ca$h Presents. Send in the first three chapters, written or typed, of your completed manuscript to:

LDP: Submissions Dept
P.O. Box 944
Stockbridge, GA 30281-9998

DO NOT send original manuscript. Must be a duplicate.
Provide your synopsis and a cover letter containing your full contact information.

Thanks for considering LDP and Ca$h Presents.

NEW RELEASES

BLOODLINE OF A SAVAGE **BY PRINCE A. TAUHID**

THE MURDER QUEENS 4 **BY MICHAEL GALLON**

THE BUTTERFLY MAFIA **BY FUMIYA PAYNE**

KING KILLA 2 **BY VINCENT "VITTO" HOLLOWAY**

BABY, I'M WINTERTIME COLD 3 **BY MEESHA**

THESE VICIOUS STREETS **BY PRINCE A. TAUHID**

TIL DEATH 2 **BY ARYANNA**

CITY OF SMOKE 2 **BY MOLOTTI**

STEPPERS **BY KING RIO**

THE LANE **BY KEN-KEN SPENCE**

MONEY GAME 2 **BY SMOOVE DOLLA**

THE BLACK DIAMOND CARTEL **BY SAYNOMORE**

CRIME BOSS 2 **BY PLAYA RAY**

THUG OF SPADES **BY COREY ROBINSON**

LOVE IN THE TRENCHES 2 **BY COREY ROBINSON**

TIL DEATH 3 **BY ARYANNA**

THE BIRTH OF A GANGSTER 4 **BY DELMONT PLAYER**

PRODUCT OF THE STREETS **BY DEMOND "MONEY" ANDERSON**

Coming Soon from Lock Down Publications/Ca$h Presents

BLOOD OF A BOSS VI
SHADOWS OF THE GAME II
TRAP BASTARD II
By **Askari**

LOYAL TO THE GAME IV
By **T.J. & Jelissa**

TRUE SAVAGE VIII
MIDNIGHT CARTEL IV
DOPE BOY MAGIC IV
CITY OF KINGZ III
NIGHTMARE ON SILENT AVE II
THE PLUG OF LIL MEXICO II
CLASSIC CITY II
By **Chris Green**

BLAST FOR ME III
A SAVAGE DOPEBOY III
CUTTHROAT MAFIA III
DUFFLE BAG CARTEL VII
HEARTLESS GOON VI
By **Ghost**

A HUSTLER'S DECEIT III
KILL ZONE II
BAE BELONGS TO ME III
TIL DEATH II
By **Aryanna**

KING OF THE TRAP III
By **T.J. Edwards**

GORILLAZ IN THE BAY V
3X KRAZY III
STRAIGHT BEAST MODE III
By **De'Kari**

KINGPIN KILLAZ IV
STREET KINGS III
PAID IN BLOOD III
CARTEL KILLAZ IV
DOPE GODS III
By **Hood Rich**

SINS OF A HUSTLA II
By **ASAD**

YAYO V
BRED IN THE GAME 2
By **S. Allen**

THE STREETS WILL TALK II
By **Yolanda Moore**

SON OF A DOPE FIEND III
HEAVEN GOT A GHETTO III
SKI MASK MONEY III
By **Renta**

LOYALTY AIN'T PROMISED III
By **Keith Williams**

I'M NOTHING WITHOUT HIS LOVE II
SINS OF A THUG II
TO THE THUG I LOVED BEFORE II
IN A HUSTLER I TRUST II
By **Monet Dragun**

QUIET MONEY IV
EXTENDED CLIP III
THUG LIFE IV
By **Trai'Quan**

THE STREETS MADE ME IV
By **Larry D. Wright**

IF YOU CROSS ME ONCE III
ANGEL V
By **Anthony Fields**

THE STREETS WILL NEVER CLOSE IV
By **K'ajji**

HARD AND RUTHLESS III
KILLA KOUNTY IV
By **Khufu**

MONEY GAME III
By **Smoove Dolla**

MURDA WAS THE CASE III
Elijah R. Freeman

AN UNFORESEEN LOVE IV
BABY, I'M WINTERTIME COLD III
By **Meesha**

QUEEN OF THE ZOO III
By **Black Migo**

CONFESSIONS OF A JACKBOY III
By **Nicholas Lock**

JACK BOYS VS DOPE BOYS IV
A GANGSTA'S QUR'AN V
COKE GIRLZ II
COKE BOYS II
LIFE OF A SAVAGE V
CHI'RAQ GANGSTAS V
SOSA GANG III
BRONX SAVAGES II
BODYMORE KINGPINS II
By **Romell Tukes**

KING KILLA II
By **Vincent "Vitto" Holloway**

BETRAYAL OF A THUG III
By **Fre$h**

THE MURDER QUEENS III
By **Michael Gallon**

THE BIRTH OF A GANGSTER III
By **Delmont Player**

TREAL LOVE II
By **Le'Monica Jackson**

FOR THE LOVE OF BLOOD III
By **Jamel Mitchell**

RAN OFF ON DA PLUG II
By **Paper Boi Rari**

HOOD CONSIGLIERE III
By **Keese**

PRETTY GIRLS DO NASTY THINGS II
By **Nicole Goosby**

PROTÉGÉ OF A LEGEND III
LOVE IN THE TRENCHES II
By **Corey Robinson**

IT'S JUST ME AND YOU II
By **Ah'Million**

FOREVER GANGSTA III
By **Adrian Dulan**

GORILLAZ IN THE TRENCHES II
By **SayNoMore**

THE COCAINE PRINCESS VIII
By **King Rio**

CRIME BOSS II
By **Playa Ray**

LOYALTY IS EVERYTHING III
By **Molotti**

HERE TODAY GONE TOMORROW II
By **Fly Rock**

A THUG'S STREET PRINCESS 2 | MEESHA

REAL G'S MOVE IN SILENCE II
By **Von Diesel**

GRIMEY WAYS IV
By **Ray Vinci**

Available Now

RESTRAINING ORDER I & II
By **CA$H & Coffee**

LOVE KNOWS NO BOUNDARIES I II & III
By **Coffee**

RAISED AS A GOON I, II, III & IV
BRED BY THE SLUMS I, II, III
BLAST FOR ME I & II
ROTTEN TO THE CORE I II III
A BRONX TALE I, II, III
DUFFLE BAG CARTEL I II III IV V VI
HEARTLESS GOON I II III IV V
A SAVAGE DOPEBOY I II
DRUG LORDS I II III
CUTTHROAT MAFIA I II
KING OF THE TRENCHES
By **Ghost**

LAY IT DOWN I & II
LAST OF A DYING BREED I II
BLOOD STAINS OF A SHOTTA I & II III
By **Jamaica**

LOYAL TO THE GAME I II III
LIFE OF SIN I, II III
By **TJ & Jelissa**

IF LOVING HIM IS WRONG…I & II
LOVE ME EVEN WHEN IT HURTS I II III
By **Jelissa**

A THUG'S STREET PRINCESS 2 | MEESHA

BLOODY COMMAS I & II
SKI MASK CARTEL I, II & III
KING OF NEW YORK I II, III IV V
RISE TO POWER I II III
COKE KINGS I II III IV V
BORN HEARTLESS I II III IV
KING OF THE TRAP I II
By **T.J. Edwards**

WHEN THE STREETS CLAP BACK I & II III
THE HEART OF A SAVAGE I II III IV
MONEY MAFIA I II
LOYAL TO THE SOIL I II III
By **Jibril Williams**

A DISTINGUISHED THUG STOLE MY HEART I II &
III
LOVE SHOULDN'T HURT I II III IV
RENEGADE BOYS I II III IV
PAID IN KARMA I II III
SAVAGE STORMS I II III
AN UNFORESEEN LOVE I II III
BABY, I'M WINTERTIME COLD I II
By **Meesha**

A GANGSTER'S CODE I &, II III
A GANGSTER'S SYN I II III
THE SAVAGE LIFE I II III
CHAINED TO THE STREETS I II III
BLOOD ON THE MONEY I II III
A GANGSTA'S PAIN I II III
By **J-Blunt**

PUSH IT TO THE LIMIT
By **Bre' Hayes**

BLOOD OF A BOSS I, II, III, IV, V
SHADOWS OF THE GAME
TRAP BASTARD
By **Askari**

THE STREETS BLEED MURDER I, II & III
THE HEART OF A GANGSTA I II& III
By **Jerry Jackson**

CUM FOR ME I II III IV V VI VII VIII
An **LDP Erotica Collaboration**

BRIDE OF A HUSTLA I II & II
THE FETTI GIRLS I, II& III
CORRUPTED BY A GANGSTA I, II III, IV
BLINDED BY HIS LOVE
THE PRICE YOU PAY FOR LOVE I, II ,III
DOPE GIRL MAGIC I II III
By **Destiny Skai**

WHEN A GOOD GIRL GOES BAD
By **Adrienne**

A GANGSTER'S REVENGE I II III & IV
THE BOSS MAN'S DAUGHTERS I II III IV V
A SAVAGE LOVE I & II
BAE BELONGS TO ME I II
A HUSTLER'S DECEIT I, II, III
WHAT BAD BITCHES DO I, II, III
SOUL OF A MONSTER I II III
KILL ZONE
A DOPE BOY'S QUEEN I II III
TIL DEATH
By **Aryanna**

THE COST OF LOYALTY I II III
By Kweli

A KINGPIN'S AMBITION
A KINGPIN'S AMBITION **II**
I MURDER FOR THE DOUGH
By **Ambitious**

TRUE SAVAGE I II III IV V VI VII
DOPE BOY MAGIC I, II, III
MIDNIGHT CARTEL I II III
CITY OF KINGZ I II
NIGHTMARE ON SILENT AVE
THE PLUG OF LIL MEXICO II
CLASSIC CITY
By **Chris Green**

A DOPEBOY'S PRAYER
By **Eddie "Wolf" Lee**

THE KING CARTEL I, II & III
By **Frank Gresham**

THESE NIGGAS AIN'T LOYAL I, II & III
By **Nikki Tee**

GANGSTA SHYT I II &III
By **CATO**

THE ULTIMATE BETRAYAL
By **Phoenix**

BOSS'N UP I, II & III
By **Royal Nicole**

I LOVE YOU TO DEATH
By **Destiny J**

I RIDE FOR MY HITTA
I STILL RIDE FOR MY HITTA
By **Misty Holt**

LOVE & CHASIN' PAPER
By **Qay Crockett**

TO DIE IN VAIN
SINS OF A HUSTLA
By **ASAD**

BROOKLYN HUSTLAZ
By **Boogsy Morina**

BROOKLYN ON LOCK I & II
By **Sonovia**

GANGSTA CITY
By **Teddy Duke**

A DRUG KING AND HIS DIAMOND I & II III
A DOPEMAN'S RICHES
HER MAN, MINE'S TOO I, II
CASH MONEY HO'S
THE WIFEY I USED TO BE I II
PRETTY GIRLS DO NASTY THINGS
By Nicole Goosby

LIPSTICK KILLAH I, II, III
CRIME OF PASSION I II & III
FRIEND OR FOE I II III
By **Mimi**

TRAPHOUSE KING I II & III
KINGPIN KILLAZ I II III
STREET KINGS I II
PAID IN BLOOD I II
CARTEL KILLAZ I II III
DOPE GODS I II
By **Hood Rich**

STEADY MOBBN' I, II, III
THE STREETS STAINED MY SOUL I II III
By **Marcellus Allen**

WHO SHOT YA I, II, III
SON OF A DOPE FIEND I II
HEAVEN GOT A GHETTO I II
SKI MASK MONEY I II
By **Renta**

GORILLAZ IN THE BAY I II III IV
TEARS OF A GANGSTA I II
3X KRAZY I II
STRAIGHT BEAST MODE I II
By **DE'KARI**

TRIGGADALE I II III
MURDA WAS THE CASE I II
By **Elijah R. Freeman**

THE STREETS ARE CALLING
By **Duquie Wilson**

SLAUGHTER GANG I II III
RUTHLESS HEART I II III
By **Willie Slaughter**

GOD BLESS THE TRAPPERS I, II, III
THESE SCANDALOUS STREETS I, II, III
FEAR MY GANGSTA I, II, III IV, V
THESE STREETS DON'T LOVE NOBODY I, II
BURY ME A G I, II, III, IV, V
A GANGSTA'S EMPIRE I, II, III, IV
THE DOPEMAN'S BODYGAURD I II
THE REALEST KILLAZ I II III
THE LAST OF THE OGS I II III
By **Tranay Adams**

MARRIED TO A BOSS I II III
By **Destiny Skai & Chris Green**

KINGZ OF THE GAME I II III IV V VI VII
CRIME BOSS
By **Playa Ray**

FUK SHYT
By **Blakk Diamond**

DON'T F#CK WITH MY HEART I II
By **Linnea**

ADDICTED TO THE DRAMA I II III
IN THE ARM OF HIS BOSS II
By **Jamila**

YAYO I II III IV
A SHOOTER'S AMBITION I II
BRED IN THE GAME
By **S. Allen**

LOYALTY AIN'T PROMISED I II
By **Keith Williams**

TRAP GOD I II III
RICH $AVAGE I II III
MONEY IN THE GRAVE I II III
By **Martell Troublesome Bolden**

FOREVER GANGSTA I II
GLOCKS ON SATIN SHEETS I II
By **Adrian Dulan**

TOE TAGZ I II III IV
LEVELS TO THIS SHYT I II
IT'S JUST ME AND YOU
By **Ah'Million**

KINGPIN DREAMS I II III
RAN OFF ON DA PLUG
By **Paper Boi Rari**

CONFESSIONS OF A GANGSTA I II III IV
CONFESSIONS OF A JACKBOY I II
By **Nicholas Lock**

I'M NOTHING WITHOUT HIS LOVE
SINS OF A THUG
TO THE THUG I LOVED BEFORE
A GANGSTA SAVED XMAS
IN A HUSTLER I TRUST
By **Monet Dragun**

QUIET MONEY I II III
THUG LIFE I II III
EXTENDED CLIP I II
A GANGSTA'S PARADISE
By **Trai'Quan**

CAUGHT UP IN THE LIFE I II III
THE STREETS NEVER LET GO I II III
By **Robert Baptiste**

NEW TO THE GAME I II III
MONEY, MURDER & MEMORIES I II III
By **Malik D. Rice**

CREAM I II III
THE STREETS WILL TALK
By **Yolanda Moore**

LIFE OF A SAVAGE I II III IV
A GANGSTA'S QUR'AN I II III IV
MURDA SEASON I II III
GANGLAND CARTEL I II III
CHI'RAQ GANGSTAS I II III IV
KILLERS ON ELM STREET I II III
JACK BOYZ N DA BRONX I II III
A DOPEBOY'S DREAM I II III
JACK BOYS VS DOPE BOYS I II III
COKE GIRLZ
COKE BOYS
SOSA GANG I II
BRONX SAVAGES
BODYMORE KINGPINS
By **Romell Tukes**

THE STREETS MADE ME I II III
By **Larry D. Wright**

CONCRETE KILLA I II III
VICIOUS LOYALTY I II III
By **Kingpen**

THE ULTIMATE SACRIFICE I, II, III, IV, V, VI
KHADIFI
IF YOU CROSS ME ONCE I II
ANGEL I II III IV
IN THE BLINK OF AN EYE
By **Anthony Fields**

THE LIFE OF A HOOD STAR
By **Ca$h & Rashia Wilson**

THE STREETS WILL NEVER CLOSE I II III
By **K'ajji**

NIGHTMARES OF A HUSTLA I II III
By **King Dream**

HARD AND RUTHLESS I II
MOB TOWN 251
THE BILLIONAIRE BENTLEYS I II III
REAL G'S MOVE IN SILENCE
By **Von Diesel**

GHOST MOB
By **Stilloan Robinson**

MOB TIES I II III IV V VI
SOUL OF A HUSTLER, HEART OF A KILLER I II
GORILLAZ IN THE TRENCHES
By **SayNoMore**

BODYMORE MURDERLAND I II III
THE BIRTH OF A GANGSTER I II
By **Delmont Player**

FOR THE LOVE OF A BOSS
By **C. D. Blue**

KILLA KOUNTY I II III IV
By Khufu

MOBBED UP I II III IV
THE BRICK MAN I II III IV V
THE COCAINE PRINCESS I II III IV V VI VII
By **King Rio**

MONEY GAME I II
By **Smoove Dolla**

A GANGSTA'S KARMA I II III
By **FLAME**

KING OF THE TRENCHES I II III
By **GHOST & TRANAY ADAMS**

QUEEN OF THE ZOO I II
By **Black Migo**

GRIMEY WAYS I II III
By **Ray Vinci**

XMAS WITH AN ATL SHOOTER
By **Ca$h & Destiny Skai**

KING KILLA
By **Vincent "Vitto" Holloway**

BETRAYAL OF A THUG I II
By **Fre$h**

A THUG'S STREET PRINCESS 2 | MEESHA

THE MURDER QUEENS I II
By **Michael Gallon**

TREAL LOVE
By **Le'Monica Jackson**

FOR THE LOVE OF BLOOD I II
By **Jamel Mitchell**

HOOD CONSIGLIERE I II
By **Keese**

PROTÉGÉ OF A LEGEND I II
LOVE IN THE TRENCHES
By **Corey Robinson**

BORN IN THE GRAVE I II III
By **Self Made Tay**

MOAN IN MY MOUTH
By **XTASY**

TORN BETWEEN A GANGSTER AND A
GENTLEMAN
By **J-BLUNT & Miss Kim**

LOYALTY IS EVERYTHING I II
By **Molotti**

HERE TODAY GONE TOMORROW
By **Fly Rock**

PILLOW PRINCESS
By **S. Hawkins**

SANCTIFIED AND HORNY
by **XTASY**

THE PLUG OF LIL MEXICO 2
by **CHRIS GREEN**

THE BLACK DIAMOND CARTEL
by **SAYNOMORE**

THE BIRTH OF A GANGSTER 3
by **DELMONT PLAYER**

BOOKS BY LDP'S CEO, CA$H

TRUST IN NO MAN
TRUST IN NO MAN 2
TRUST IN NO MAN 3
BONDED BY BLOOD
SHORTY GOT A THUG
THUGS CRY
THUGS CRY 2
THUGS CRY 3
TRUST NO BITCH
TRUST NO BITCH 2
TRUST NO BITCH 3
TIL MY CASKET DROPS
RESTRAINING ORDER
RESTRAINING ORDER 2
IN LOVE WITH A CONVICT
LIFE OF A HOOD STAR
XMAS WITH AN ATL SHOOTER